THE ARTIST OF DISAPPEARANCE

The Artist of Disappearance

Three Novellas

❖

Anita Desai

Chatto & Windus
LONDON

Published by Chatto & Windus 2011

2 4 6 8 10 9 7 5 3 1

First published in Great Britain in 2011 by
Chatto & Windus
Random House, 20 Vauxhall Bridge Road,
London SW1V 2SA
www.randomhouse.co.uk

Text design by Lindsay Nash

Addresses for companies within The Random House Group Limited
can be found at: www.randomhouse.co.uk/offices.htm

The Random House Group Limited Reg. No. 954009

A CIP catalogue record for this book
is available from the British Library

ISBN 9780701186203

The Random House Group Limited supports The Forest Stewardship
Council® (FSC®), the leading international forest certification organisation.
All our titles that are printed on Greenpeace approved FSC® certified paper
carry the FSC® logo. Our paper procurement policy can be found at
www.randomhouse.co.uk/environment

Typeset in Bembo by Palimpsest Book Production Limited, Falkirk, Stirlingshire
Printed and bound in Great Britain by
CPI Mackays, Chatham ME5 8TD

For my brother
Dinu Mazumdar
I owe him much

One thing alone does not exist – oblivion.

– 'Everness', Jorge Luis Borges
translated by Alastair Reid

CONTENTS

The Museum of Final Journeys

WE HAD DRIVEN for never-ending miles along what seemed to be more a mudbank than a road between fields of virulent green – jute? rice? what was it this benighted hinterland produced? I ought to have known, but my head was pounded into too much of a daze by the heat and the sun and the fatigue to take in what my driver was telling me in answer to my listless questions.

The sun was setting into a sullen murk of ashes and embers along the horizon when he turned the jeep into the circular driveway in front of a low, white bungalow. This was the circuit house where I was to stay until I had found a place of my own. As a very junior officer, a mere subdivisional officer in the august government service, it was all I could expect, a temporary place for one of its minor servants. There was nothing around but fields and dirt roads and dust, no lights or signs of a town to be seen. Noting my disappointment and hesitation at the first sight of my new residence – where had we come to? – the driver climbed out first, lifted my bags from the back of the jeep and led the way up the broad steps to a long veranda which had doors fitted with wire screens one could not see through. He clapped his hands and shouted, 'Koi hai?' I had not imagined anyone still used that imperious announcement from the days of the Raj: Anyone there? But perhaps, in this setting, itself a leftover from the empire, not so incongruous at all. Besides, there was no bell and one cannot knock on a screen door.

I didn't think anyone had heard. Certainly no light went on and no footsteps were to be heard, but in a bit someone came around the house from the back where there must have been huts or quarters for servants.

'I've brought the new officer-sahib,' the driver announced officiously (he wore a uniform of sorts, khaki, with lettering in red over the shirt pocket that gave him the right). 'Open a room for him. And switch on some lights, will you?'

'No lights,' the man replied with dignity. He wore no uniform, only some loose clothing, and his feet were bare, but he held his back straight and somehow established his authority. 'Power cut.'

'Get a lantern then,' the driver barked. He clearly enjoyed giving orders.

I didn't, and was relieved when the chowkidar – for clearly he was the watchman for all his lack of a uniform – took over my bags and the driver turned to leave. It was night now, and when I saw the headlights of the jeep sweep over the dark foliage that crowded against the house and lined the driveway, then turn around so that the tail lights could be seen to dwindle and disappear, I felt my heart sinking. I did not want to stay in this desolate place, I wanted to run after the jeep, throw myself in and return to a familiar scene. I was used to city life, to the cacophony of traffic, the clamour and din and discordancy of human voices, the pushing and shoving of humanity, all that was absent here.

While I stood waiting on the veranda for a lamp to be lit so I could be shown to my room, I listened to the dry, grating crackle of palm leaves over the roof, the voices of frogs issuing low warnings from some invisible pond or swamp nearby, and these sounds were even more disquieting than the silence.

A lighted lantern was finally brought out and I followed its ghostly glow in, past large, looming pieces of furniture, to the room the chowkidar opened for me. It released a dank odour of mildew as of a trunk opened after a long stretch of time and a death or two, and I thought this was surely not a chapter of my life; it was only a chapter in one of those novels I used to read in my student days, something by Robert Louis Stevenson or Arthur Conan Doyle or Wilkie Collins (I had been a great reader then and secretly hoped to become a writer). I remembered, too, the hated voice of the gym master at school shouting 'Stiffen up now, boys, stiffen up!' and I nearly laughed – a bitter laugh.

All the actions that one performs automatically and habitually in the real world, the lighted world – of bathing, dressing, eating a meal – here had to be performed in a state of almost gelid slow motion. I carried the lantern into the bathroom with me – it created grotesquely hovering shadows rather than light, and made the slimy walls and floor glisten dangerously – and made do with a rudimentary bucket of water and a tin mug. To put on a clean set of clothes when I could scarcely make out what I had picked from my suitcase (packed with an idiotic lack of good sense: a tie? when would I ever wear a tie in this pit?) and then to find my way to the dining room and sit down to a meal placed before me that I could scarcely identify – was it lentils, or a mush of vegetables, and was this whitish puddle rice or what? – all were manoeuvres to be carried out with slow deliberation, so much so that they seemed barely worthwhile, just habits belonging to another world and time carried on weakly. The high-pitched whining of mosquitoes sounded all around me and I slapped angrily at their invisible presences.

Then, with a small explosion, the electricity came on and lights flared with an intensity that made me flinch. An abrupt shift took place. The circuit house dining room, the metal bowls and dishes set on the table, the heavy pieces of furniture, the yellow curry stains on the tablecloth all revealed themselves with painful clarity while the whine of mosquitoes faded with disappointment. Now large, winged ants insinuated their way through the wire screens and hurled themselves at the electric bulb suspended over my head; some floated down into my plate where they drowned in the gravy, wings detaching themselves from the small, floundering worms of their bodies.

I pushed back my chair and rose so precipitately, the chowkidar came forward to see what was wrong. I saw no point in telling him that everything was. Instructing him abruptly to bring me tea at six next morning, I returned to my room. It felt like a mercy to turn off the impudent light dangling on a cord over my bed and prepare to throw myself into it for the night.

I had not taken the mosquito net that swaddled the bed into account. First I had to fumble around for an opening to crawl in, then tuck it back to keep out the mosquitoes. At this I failed, and those that found themselves trapped in the netting with me, furiously bit at every exposed surface they could find. What was more, the netting prevented any breath of air reaching me from the sluggishly revolving fan overhead.

Throughout the night voices rang back and forth in my head: would I be able to go through with this training in a remote outpost that was supposed to prepare me for great deeds in public service? Should I quit now before I became known as a failure and a disgrace? Could I appeal to anyone for help, some mentor, or possibly my father, retired now from this very service, his honour and his pride intact like an iron rod he had swallowed?

Across the jungle, or the swamp or whatever it was that surrounded this isolated house, pai dogs in hamlets and home-steads scattered far apart echoed the voices in my head, some questioning and plaintive, others fierce and challenging.

If I had not been 'stiffened up' in school and by my father, I might have shed a tear or two into my flat grey pillow. I came close to it but morning rescued me.

★　★　★

I resolved to look for another, more amenable place to live during my posting here, but soon had to admit that the chance of finding such a place was very unlikely. The town, if you could call it that, was not one where people built houses with the intention of selling or renting them for profit; its citizens built for the purpose of housing their families till they fell apart. Many of the houses were embarked on that inexorable process, larger and larger families crowding into smaller and smaller spaces while roofs collapsed and walls crumbled. Families did not move even when forced onto verandas or into outhouses. The whole town appeared a shambles.

It must have had its days of prosperity in the past when the jute that grew thick and strong in the surrounding fields gave rise to a flourishing business, but that was now overtaken by chemical fibres, plastics and polyesters. Their products – the bags, washing lines, buckets and basins that hung from shopfronts – littered the dusty streets where their strident colours soon faded.

Every morning I went to court, a crumbling structure of red brick that stood in a field where cattle grazed and wash-ermen spread their washing, and there I sat at a desk on a slightly raised platform to hear the cases brought before me. These had chiefly to do with disputes over property. You would not have thought the local property was anything to be fought over but the citizens of this district were devoted to litigation with an ardour not evident in any other area of life. A wall that had caved in or two coconut trees that had not borne fruit for as long as anyone could remember, even

8

these aroused the passion of ownership. I began to see it as the one local industry. I took back files with me to read in the evenings on the veranda of the circuit house while the power cuts held off.

In my office in the administrative buildings, I attended to more urgent matters like power and water supplies and their frequent breakdowns, roads, traffic, police – very important that, the police force – communications, security, trade and industry. (The litigators, and especially their lawyers, were always willing to have their cases postponed from one hearing to the next.) My secretary brought in the files to me, tied with red tape – I was amused to see these existed, literally – and ushered in visitors with their requests, demands and complaints. I would order tea for them, but try as I would, I could never have tea, sugar and milk served in separate pots as my mother would have: these would always arrive already mixed in the cups, and for some reason this irritated me greatly and I never ceased to complain about it.

I must have complained in my letters to my mother, too, because she worried that I was not being looked after as I would be at home. She even made efforts to find a bride for me, convinced that a wife was what I needed, a woman who would order my life and make it comfortable and pleasant for me. I was lonely enough not to discourage her, even though the idea of some stranger entering my life in such an intimate fashion did somewhat alarm me. No such thing came to pass, however. When my father discovered she was interviewing the unmarried daughters and nieces of her friends and acquaintances, dangling my position in the Civil Service and my prospects for promotions to high and important posts in the future as incentives, he put a stop to all such machinations: there was to be no marriage till my training was over and confirmation in the service achieved.

In a very short time the routine of my working life became oppressive. When I entered the service it was with the thought that it would be an endless adventure, and each day would bring fresh challenges and demand new solutions. My father and my senior colleagues had all assured me it would be so. They talked of their own adventures – shooting man-eaters that had terrorised the locals and 'lifted' their cattle, confronting dacoits who had been robbing travellers on highways, hunting down 'criminal elements' that dealt in smuggling goods or illicit liquor, and, most threatening of all, instigators of political insurgencies. To me these remained rumours, legends, and I came to suspect that my leg had been pulled. *My* most strenuous activity seemed to be wielding the fly-swatter and mopping my face in the thick damp heat that clung like wet clothing in the most debilitating way.

There was the occasional visitor to the circuit house: another officer on a tour of duty would stop for a night on his way to inspect the waterworks or the sewage plant or the government-run clinic or school or whatever he happened to be in charge of, and leave the next day, having provided me with one evening of company. Since all we had to talk about was the business at hand, these visits did not provide me with the much needed diversion.

The only release to be had was to find an excuse to go 'on tour', summon my jeep and driver and make for the further reaches of the district. At its northern rim was tea country and the sight of that trim landscape of tea bushes and shade trees on softly rolling hills that rose eventually into the blue mountain range – alas, not my territory – was as reviving as a drink of cool water to me.

Seated in the ample cane furniture on the broad veranda of one fortunate tea-estate manager's bungalow over a whisky and soda, I could not help a sigh of relief tinged with melancholy that this salubrious place was not mine and I would soon have to return to my sorry posting below.

My host enquired how I was faring. When I told him – I admit with an openly pathetic plea for sympathy – he said, 'I know the town. I have to visit it from time to time. It doesn't even have a club, does it?'

'No! If only there were a club where I could play tennis after work . . .' I gave another sigh, drawn out of me by his evident sympathy.

'No social life either?'

'There's no one I could have a conversation with about *anything* but work. There's no library or anyone who reads. I'm running out of books too.'

My host got up to pour me another peg at the bar constructed of bamboo at the other end of the spacious veranda. My eyes followed him, admiring the polished floor, the pots of ferns that lined the steps and the orchids that hung in baskets above them.

When he returned to his seat, he handed me my drink and said, 'In the old days there used to be wealthy Calcutta families who owned land around here and who would come to visit it from time to time, throw parties and organise hunts. Of course, those times are over and their estates must have gone to rack and ruin by now.'

We talked a bit longer about this and that till I had to leave, and as I walked past the open door on my way to the steps and stood waiting for my jeep to be driven round to the front, my eye fell on a small object on the hall table – two small Chinese figures in flowered tunics and black slippers carrying a kind of palanquin between them. It was both unusual and pretty and I looked at it more closely: the details were exquisite and there was a gloss to it such as you see on the finest china. My host saw me lingering to study it and said, 'Oh, it's one of those objects one sometimes comes across in these parts that belonged to the old houses I was telling you about. One of them even had a museum once: perhaps this came from there. My wife picked it up, she has an eye for such things. I told her she had paid too much – it's only a wind-up toy, you know, and has lost its key.'

'A wind-up toy!' I exclaimed. 'It looks too precious for that. Is it very old?'

'I couldn't tell you, I don't know a thing about it. It's a pity my wife is in Shillong – our daughters are at school there – she would have been able to tell you more.'

'Beautiful,' I said, and reluctantly took my leave.

I can't say I gave that beautiful object or its provenance any more thought. Inevitably, I grew more involved in my work and had to see through various projects I had started on as well as the daily routine of attending court to hear cases that grew drearily familiar, and going through the bottomless stack of files in my office. I even stopped asking for milk and sugar to be brought separately for my tea and resigned myself to drinking the thick, murky liquid I was served.

I became so settled in a state of apathy – it was like an infection I had caught from those around me – that I felt quite irritated when the chowkidar at the circuit house roused me from it one evening as I sat slumped in the reclining chair under the revolving fan in my room, waiting for darkness to fall and for him to call me to my dinner.

Instead he said, 'Someone to see you, sahib.'

'Who?' I snapped, and added, 'Tell him to come and see me in my office tomorrow. I don't see visitors here.'

'That is right, sahib,' the chowkidar acknowledged, 'but he has come from far and says it is a matter he needs to discuss privately.'

'What matter?' I snapped again (I had acquired this habitual manner of speech to those in an inferior position – servants, petitioners, supplicants; I found it was expected of me, it went with the job).

13

Of course the chowkidar could not know or tell. He stood there expecting some action from me, so, with a show of petulance, I threw down the newspaper folded to the crossword puzzle that I had been pretending to solve, and went out to the veranda where the visitor stood waiting: an elderly, rather bowed man with wisps of white hair showing under his cap like feathers, enormous spectacles with thick lenses and heavy frames attached to him by string, and dressed in a faded black cloth coat and close white trousers, perhaps the outfit he had adopted as a clerk (he had the obsequious manner of one) before his superannuation.

Some remnant of my upbringing surfaced through my adopted manner of irritable superiority (from behind my father's looming shadow, my mother occasionally emerged to stand watching me, hopefully, trustingly). I gestured to him to be seated and called to the chowkidar to bring us water. Just that, pani.

The clerical creature folded his hands and asked me not to bother. 'I am deeply sorry to disturb your rest,' he said in a voice just slightly above the whine of a mosquito, perhaps closer to the sound of a small cricket.

I found my habitual annoyance beginning to creep back and said abruptly, 'What can I do for you?'

'Sir, I have come from the Mukherjee estate thirty-five miles from here,' the poor man brought out as if embarrassed to make a statement that might sound boastful. Why should it? I wondered, and waited. 'I have served the family for fifty years,' he went on, barely above a whisper, and kept touching, nerv-ously, his small white beard like a goat's — a goatee.

'I don't know the place,' I told him.

'Sir, it was once the largest estate in the district,' he said imploringly, seeing that I needed to be persuaded. 'The family owned fields of jute and rice and even tea and cinchona in the north. Also coal mines. Many properties in the district belonged to them. They were rented out. It was my duty to keep account of it all. In those days I had many assistants, it was too much for me to handle alone. My father had served before me and I was employed by the family when I was still a boy. They trusted my family and they put it all in my hands.'

This was going to be a long story, I realised, if I was to allow him to unfold it at this pace. We might need to travel backwards to generations now long gone, pallid ghosts disap-pearing one after the other into the dark night of the past. When would we arrive in the daylight of the present? I wondered, sitting up with a jerk to accept a glass of water from the chowkidar and hoping by my brisk action to indicate that my time was valuable and it was running out.

But, like a mosquito that has got under one's net and can't be driven out, the ancient gnome went on murmuring, and the tale he had to tell was exactly the one I had feared: the usual saga of a descent from riches to rags, the property fragmenting as the sons of one generation quarrelled and insisted on ill-judged divisions, the gradual crumbling of wealth as tenant farmers failed to pay rent, and litigation that never led to solutions, only protracted the death throes. Then the house itself, the one the family had occupied while it multiplied, falling down piecemeal, the cost of repair and maintenance making its eventual disintegration inevitable.

The familiar story of the fabled zamindars of old. I could have recited any number of them to this poor, whispering ancient who seemed to think his was the only such story to be told.

But at some point – perhaps I had dozed off briefly, then woken – I began to hear what he was saying. It was the word 'museum' that had the effect of a mosquito bite after a long spell of droning.

'The museum at our house was started by Srimati Sarita Mukherjee who was married to my master in the year 19— when she was thirteen and he sixty years of age. She was the second wife of Sri Bhupen Mukherjee who inherited the property from his father Debabrata Mukherjee in 19—. He had no issue from his first marriage. Srimati Sarita Devi was of the Sinha family that resides in Serampore. The family was wealthy and accordingly she brought with her a substantial dowry. It was not so large in property as in gold and gems. The family was known for its love of art and literature and she had grown up in the company of educated men and women and had some education herself.

'It was not easy for her to adjust to the life on our estate, which is not only a great distance from her home but far from any other estate in our district. Sri Bhupen Mukherjee, being an only son, had no brothers or sisters-in-law who might have provided her with some company. Naturally she had many lonely years as the only lady in the house. Then, when she was nineteen years of age, a son was born to her. Sri Jiban Mukherjee gave us all joy as he was the natural heir and we had great hopes he would keep the estate intact and make it prosper. Sadly, Sri Bhupen Mukherjee did not live much longer and could take pride in his heir for only a few short years before he expired. So my duty became very clear to me: I had to make sure that the inheritance that came to the young boy would be substantial and he and his mother would lack for nothing.'

At this point I found my knee beginning to jog involuntarily up and down. I am sure it was because I was growing impatient to learn: did *she* create a museum? Did it exist?

'Then we had a number of bad years in a row when the rains did not come and the crops were ruined and our coal mines suffered one disaster after another and had to be abandoned. For several years the estate had no income at all, only losses. There was no money available for repairs and maintenance. We were forced to take loans simply to keep the place running and we fell into debt.

'Times did improve but whatever income there was had to be spent on paying off debts. It was sad to see Srimati Sarita Devi's face so careworn and her hair turn grey before her time. She was burdened with worry not only with regard to finances but also to her son Sri Jiban's upbringing and education of which she had sole responsibility after the death of his father.'

At this point the narrator paused. He seemed crushed by the sadness of what he had to relate. I found I had become involved with it in spite of myself and so had to allow him to unfold the tale at his own pace which was slow but persistent. Having run out of books to read, even so slight and familiar a story as I was hearing now had enough interest to keep me from seeing off this unwelcome insect of a visitor.

'I am sorry to say she had to sell her gold and jewellery bit by bit to pay for his education as the estate itself could not bear the expense. She saw to it that he was sent to the best school in Calcutta, one run by the Jesuit fathers, and there-after to university in England as his father would have wished. We had great hopes that on his return with a degree in law, he would set up a successful practice as a barrister so that he could support his mother in the manner to which she was born.'

His voice had grown so low that it seemed to mimic the dusk into which the circuit house, its veranda and the surrounding wilderness had sunk, leaving us in darkness, and for a while I could barely hear him at all, but perhaps that was because the chowkidar had arrived with a mosquito coil which he lit to drive away the mosquitoes now beginning to swarm, then went indoors to pump a Flit gun vigorously for the same purpose, and finally turned on the lights. He also coughed repeatedly, in a blatantly false manner, to signal it was time for my visitor to leave so he could serve me my dinner, then retire. I could interpret all these signs after my protracted stay in the circuit house but my visitor ignored him and after a few long sighs resumed his narrative.

'Unfortunately, Sri Jiban, having lived abroad for several years, could not adjust to life on our estate or even to Calcutta. He had no interest in the affairs of the estate and left it all to his mother to take care of as before. We waited to see what his plans were for the future. Naturally he did not confide in me but one day I saw him packing his bags and heard him send for a tonga to take him to the nearest railway station. His mother wept as she saw him drive away and when I attempted to console her by saying he would surely return soon, she replied she did not think he would because he was planning a long sea voyage to countries in the East. I was astounded by this information because I did not see how he could fund such an ambitious voyage; nor could I see its purpose. I then learned she had sold the last of her jewellery to finance his desire.'

I was now beginning to wonder why I was being made privy to the family's secrets. I would have risen to my feet to indicate the time I had given him was now up, but something about his posture, so crushed, his hands held tightly together as if in agony, and the way his old white head trembled on its thin stalk of a neck stopped me. Also, frankly, I wanted to know where the story would go.

To my surprise, he now lifted his head so I could see his expression more clearly by the light that fell on us from the lighted rooms within, and I saw that he looked quite serene, almost joyful.

'Then the boxes began to arrive. They came from Burma, from Thailand, from Indonesia, from Malaya, Cambodia, the Philippines and even China and Japan, containing such objects as had never been seen in our part of the world! People would come from their villages miles away to our gates to watch the bullock carts they had seen hauling these boxes to our door, and there was much talk about what they might contain.' He actually laughed at this point, a dry rustling in his throat like that made by a bird or insect in a bush, a kind of cackle you might call it. 'Our people are simple folk. They have no knowledge of the world and the countries our young master had visited but, seeing the size of the containers, they thought he was involved in trade and that he had made a fortune so he could send his mother treasures in the form of silks and jewels and other valuable goods.' He shook his head now at their foolishness and gullibility. 'They believed the young master would return a wealthy man and restore our estate,' and here his laugh ended in a small hiccup. 'We opened the containers as they came and were astonished by what we found. He had sent us few letters or messages and we could only conjecture where he had been and where he had found or purchased the goods revealed to us.'

'And –?'

'One room after the other was filled with these objects. We brought in carpenters to build glass cases and put up shelves to display them. Each container provided the contents for a different room, the rooms that had been empty for so long – we had

20

been selling items of furniture and other belongings ever since we fell upon hard times – and now they were filled again. Visitors came to the house and were astonished by what they saw. One even wished to make a catalogue of these objects and publish it to make the collection known. Srimati Sarita Devi could not tell them anything about the objects or where her son had obtained them, but they gave her great solace because they allowed her to accompany him on his voyage. Only I was perturbed: I did not see the use of such things. They were objects of beauty and interest, but what was the use of collecting them? I could not see, but Srimati Sarita Devi did. She told me, "Bijan, we are creating a great museum. My son's collection is forming a museum that people will hear about all over our land and will come from far to see."'

Ah, so there *was* a museum! I found myself growing excited to learn this had not been merely a rumour or a folk tale but actually existed. I even asked him if I could come and visit it.

At this he first closed his eyes as if in weariness, then opened them wide with a radiant gaze, and cried out, 'Sir, this is my dearest wish! Come, please come and visit us, advise me what to do! I am old now, as you see, and I do not know what will become of it once I am gone. Already people – visitors, perhaps even members of our own staff who have learned there are no guards, no security – have been removing some small objects. I have myself seen these things appearing in markets here and there. The only way open to me to keep it intact is to request the government, the sarkar, take it over and maintain it. If you come and see it for yourself, you will see how great the need is for security and support. Without it −' He broke off, as if the alternative was unthinkable, and mopped his face with a cloth he withdrew from his pocket.

But was there no alternative? Did the errant son not return to his ancestral property? What of Srimati Sarita Devi, his mother? What were her wishes in the matter? I tried to probe tactfully.

'Sir,' the unhappy man confessed, 'she left us with no instructions.'

This seemed vague to me. Had she died and 'left for her heavenly abode' as they say in the classified columns of our newspapers? Or moved out of the museum/mausoleum and left it to him? He seemed strangely unwilling to say. He had come to the end of his narrative and had, he seemed to indicate, no more to say. 'The collection' was all that was left at the end of it.

My own enthusiasm came to an abrupt halt as if it had met with an obstruction, a speed break. I began to see only too well the tangle of legal problems ahead. Not at all what I had imagined, although I should have done so. I felt let down by the realisation that it all came down to practicalities, legal and administrative. Just as if I hadn't had my fill of these. While others dreamt dreams and lived lives of imagination and adventure, my role was only to take care of the mess left by them.

My curiosity about the museum and my desire to see it were quickly evaporating. But, if they afforded me a break from the daily routine of office and courtroom in this oppressively limited outpost, why not accept? I told him I would have my driver bring me, asked for directions, and found a suitable date. His gratitude made him practically bow before me – a display of obsequiousness that was more than I could bear. I turned my head and went in to my dinner, leaving him to find his own way out.

I should have known better than to expect some miraculous Xanadu. As my jeep bumped and bounced its way along the mudbank that passed for a road between flattened fields of stubble with only an occasional coconut tree or grove of bananas beside a stagnant pond to break the monotony of a landscape bleached of colour, my expectations dwindled and sobered. The last stretch ended at what no doubt had been an imposing gateway, but now consisted of two pillars of brick with parasitic trees growing out of the cracks, and only some rusty hinges left to show where the wrought-iron gates had hung.

Ahead of us lay what had probably been the driveway but was now a grassy field in which a few skeletal cows grazed, watched over by a cowherd with a staff. He stood with one foot resting against the knee of the other leg like a flamingo blackened by the sun. His face did register some astonishment at seeing a motor vehicle make its way over the hummocky grass, but other than that he made no acknowledgement of our intrusion. And the cows merely switched their tails and flicked their ears at our passing and a few cattle egrets took off from their flanks with lazy flaps of their wings.

Having traversed the length of the field we came to what had to be 'the palace' I had come to see. What did I expect? There was a broad flight of stairs with grass growing between the flagstones, and beyond it the mournful remains of what I had been assured was once the most substantial house in the district. At first sight I could make out no architectural features in the blackened, crumbling ruin.

Only time, and dissolution.

But here came my acquaintance, the clerk/caretaker, tumbling recklessly down the irregular stairs while adjusting the cap on his head and the buttons of his long black cloth coat as if these gave him his identity and status. Yet his manner on greeting me was gracious and courtly in a way that could only be called 'cultured' or even 'aristocratic', and I felt a twinge of shame at recalling how brusquely I had dismissed him. Although, when he launched into a flowery speech of gratitude at my coming, his joy at seeing me, the honour it accorded him and the house he served, I could not help cutting him short and being curt once again. I suggested we set about doing our tour.

He insisted, however, that I first rest a little and take some refreshment. On the broad veranda spread around the rooms like a lap on which they had settled, a table had been set with an embroidered cloth and a tarnished silver tray on which was a jug, covered with a square of net edged with beads, and some tall metal tumblers. A servant boy emerged from somewhere –

a coal-hole, I conjectured – to pour out some coloured sherbet drink that I was not able to refuse.

'Bring the keys,' my host the clerk commanded, assuming the posture of one whose right it was to give orders. Before my eyes he became stiffly upright – still small of course but upright nevertheless – his mouth set in a firm line, his eyes sharp and watchful, his bearing almost arrogant. Here was a person, I saw, who was much more capable of commanding than I was. I observed him and the air with which he accepted the ring of keys from the servant boy as though they were the keys to a castle, his castle. Then, to my surprise, he held them behind his back with one hand, and with the other gestured to me to precede him through an open door. Were the keys only some part of a charade?

We entered the hall of the palace of the past between two marble – or highly polished ceramic – slave figures holding up lamps filled with dust and dead moths; they had onyx for eyes that bulged grotesquely out of their heads.

The room itself was empty except for a small marble-topped table on ornate legs, carved like dragons. Under it was what looked like a china chamber pot – but could that be? Perhaps I have imagined or misinterpreted it, and other details. On the faded, mottled walls portraits hung from long ropes and huge nails, tilting forward as if to peer down at us. They were photographs in the main but tinted by hand to look like paintings, a strange technique by which one art was imposed on another, leaving the surface oddly ambiguous. One was of a small man in a large turban who stood in front of a dead tiger with its mouth propped open in a snarl; another of a large man with whiskers that bristled like the tiger's, seated upon a gilt chair. Yet another image of perhaps the same man standing, his foot on a recently murdered elephant, a gun in his hand and a row of barely clad servants – beaters? – on either side.

And then one of a woman, scarcely more than a child, slender, her cheeks tinted pink and with strands of pearls around her neck from which hung one large gem tinted green. She wore an old-fashioned blouse with long puffed sleeves that ended in lace at the wrists, and a sari that fell in sculpted folds from her shoulders to her slippered feet, its silver trim draped over her head where her hair was parted in two wings over wide-set eyes. This was the only female portrait, and as we passed it, I heard the clerk sigh, 'Srimati Sarita Devi.' Or perhaps I imagined that because I wished it to be her, the child bride. Since he had not said 'The late Srimati' I still did not know if she was alive, somewhere in the recesses of this faded mansion, and if I would be taken to meet her, or if she was the late, departed Srimati S. My escort remained silent on the matter.

He was already showing me into an adjoining hall where the beasts slaughtered by this family had been embalmed and stuffed to look lifelike or had had their pelts removed and stretched out upon the walls under a forest of antlers and the mounted heads of glass-eyed stags. I tried to avoid looking up at them: I did not enjoy the sensation of being watched, accusingly I thought. 'The men in the family were great hunters,' my guide said, as if explanation were needed, and I could detect neither apology nor pride in his voice because he kept it as low as if we were in a mausoleum. I decided it was merely respectful so I too tried to look respectful but must have failed: my father had also been a hunter in his days and I had not liked to look on his trophies or hear about his exploits which sounded boastful and made my mother cringe. I probably looked merely blank as I stared at the scalloped and scaly skin of a crocodile or of a python, mottled and moth-like, one resembling broken rubble, the other faded netting. I turned to the clerk, who had his hands behind his back and his head uplifted to these specimens he was set here to guard, and indicated I wished to hurry on. But, before leaving this chamber of death, I had to pass a large, pot-like object by the door. From its folds and wrinkles and the massive flattened toenails, I discerned it to be the foot of an elephant. In case I missed the point of this dismemberment, some umbrellas had been placed in it, their cloth covering frayed and their tin ribs exposed.

Unfortunately the next chamber was one of stuffed birds and they did little to improve my spirits. If anything, the glass eyes set in grey sockets were even more accusing and I was certain that their faded, iridiscent feathers were creeping with parasitic life.

The only living creatures visible in these chambers were the spiders that spun their webs to make shrouds for the birds and the geckoes that probably fed on the spiders. I saw one lizard flattened against the wall, immobile, a pulse beating under its nearly transparent skin to show it was just waiting for us to leave, for night to fall, so it could come to life again. In one doorway, a gecko caught by the slam of the door had left its fragile skeleton splayed against the plaster like a web spun by one of the spiders, to stay till it peeled.

'Is this,' I demanded, 'is *this* the young master's collection?' If there was sarcasm in my tone, it was intentional.

My guide, proving aware of it, quickly responded, 'No, no, no. No, this was left to him by his ancestors. Now we will go to see *his* collection.' And, to my huge relief, we came out into a corridor completely bare of trophies, one side opening onto a courtyard where a marble goddess stood in the shallow basin of a waterless fountain. Her limbs were broken at the joints and lichen had crept up her sandalled feet to the hem of her robe. This stretch of corridor evidently led to the wing that held the items sent to the estate by the absconding master in containers that had created such a stir in the district and a legacy for the inheritors – if any.

And now my guide produced the ring of keys from behind his back because we had come to a door that was locked. Choosing one extraordinarily long key from the ring, he inserted it into the lock and turned it with a great sense of drama. I followed him in with some trepidation and impatience: how many more hunting trophies and murdered spoils was I to be shown? The heat of the day was gathering in these closed, unventilated rooms, and although it must have been noon by now, there was very little light here.

Except, I was astonished to find, what the collection itself radiated. The chamber we had entered was hung, draped, laid and overlaid with rugs in the splendid colours of royalty – plum, wine, mulberry and pomegranate – woven into intricate patterns. I hesitated to step on one, they were surely precious and, besides, had not been touched in ages by hand, still less by foot. Only a raja might recline on one, with his rani, while listening to the music of sitar and sarod, tabla and tanpura. I could imagine these invisible potentates and pashas lifting goblets in their ringed hands or, better still, the chased silver mouthpiece of a hookah. Lives lived in such a setting could only have been noble and luxurious – not of this poor, hardworked land around.

It was only when I lowered my eyes to examine them more closely that I noted what the imperial colours concealed: patches that were faded, threadbare, some even darned and mended, clumsily.

My guide watched my reactions as they flickered across my face – I'm sure my expressions gave me away – and seemed gratified, a small smile lifting the corners of his compressed lips. But before I could bend and examine more closely these Persian, Turkish, Afghan, Moroccan and Kashmiri treasures, he ushered me into the next room.

And this was even more richly rewarding, for here hung the miniature paintings of Turkey, Persia, Moghul India, Rajasthan and Kangra. I was not enough of a connoisseur to identify them and it would have taken days, even a lifetime, to examine each separately and study the clues enclosed by the gilt margins. Here were jewel-like illustrations of floral and avian life, tiny figures mounted on curvaceous horses in pursuit of lions and gazelles, or kneeling before bearded saints in mountain caves. I glimpsed a pair of cranes performing a mating dance on a green hillock before passing on to a young maiden conversing with her pet parrot in a cage and another penning a letter to a distant beloved, and so to a sly young man spying from behind a tree on a bevy of young girls bathing in a river, clothed, but transparently. Here elephants with gilded howdahs on their backs carried noblemen up bare hills to crenellated forts on the summits, and now blue storm clouds appeared, driving white egrets before them; a dancing girl performed in a walled courtyard; a prince posed with a pink rose in his hand, another proudly exhibited a hawk upon his wrist. Hunting dogs streamed after deer in a forest, a hunter following them with a bow and arrow. A ship set sail. Lightning struck. Lines of exquisite script curled through the borders, naming their names, telling their tales.

I could not read them, partly from the unfamiliarity of the scripts, but also because the glass that separated these wonderful worlds from the spectator was filmed with dust. No hand had touched them since they were framed and hung. There were no visitors to admire them, just the old caretaker who seemed more proud than knowledgeable, and I who could say nothing but 'Ah!' and 'Ahh!'

If I had been shown just these two chambers, I should have felt satisfied and certain of the value of this collection, but we did not stop here. The caretaker, bowing slightly, was showing me through the door to another chamber, this one filled with fans and kimonos. Disembodied, they contrived somehow to beckon and flirt. It was easy to imagine the fine tapered fingers that must have wielded these fans of carved ivory and pleated silk painted with scenes of gardens and festivals, or the slender figures that had worn these silk gowns, opulent and elaborate with sweeping sleeves and trailing borders of indigo and verdigris, bronze and jade, amethyst and azure. They seemed to plead for their glass cases to be opened so they might step out of these frozen tableaux and assume the roles of queens and courtesans to which they were born.

But such exposure might have revealed them to be ghosts, a touch of air might have turned them to dust. The sleeves were empty, the hems ended in no slippers and no feet. Their fans stirred no air. It occurred to me that the little toylike object, which had caught my eye in my friend the tea-estate manager's house, might once have stood among these ghosts, their plaything, before it was spirited away by some light-fingered viewer. And so they had no vehicle, not even a miniature palanquin.

I found myself invaded by their poetic melancholy and would have liked to linger, fancying myself a privileged visitor to a past world, but the caretaker gave a warning cough to remind me of his presence and our purpose in being here; I turned round to see him holding open another door to another chamber.

And so I was marched through one filled with masks of wood, straw, leather and clay, painted and embellished with bone, shells, rings, strings and fur, masks that threatened or mocked or terrified, then one of textiles – printed, woven, dyed and bleached, gauze, muslin, silk and brocade – and after that one of footwear – fantastical, foolish, foppish – followed by one of headwear – caps and bonnets of velvet, straw, net and felt . . . What kind of traveller had this been who desired and acquired the stuff of other people's lands and lives? Why did he? And how had it all arrived here to make up this preposterous collection?

The guide, smiling enigmatically, would give me no clues. Now he was showing me cases filled with weapons of war – curved swords, stout daggers, hilts engraved with decorative patterns that concealed murderous intent – and now he was glancing to see my reaction to a display of porcelain and ceramic – delicate receptacles painted with scenes of arched bridges and willow groves, mountains and waterfalls, or abstract patterns of fierce intricacy in bold and brilliant colours.

I felt sated, wanted to protest, hardly able to take in any more wonders, any more miracles, but detected a certain ruthlessness to my guide's opening of door after door, ushering me on and on, much further than I wished to go. I had thought of him as aged and frail, but his pride and determination to impress me seemed to give him a strength and stamina I would not have imagined possible and it was I who was exhausted, overcome by the heat, stopping to mop my face, even stumbling, yet also curiously unwilling to admit defeat and leave what I had undertaken incomplete.

And there was a chamber we came across every now and then that I would have gladly lingered in, the chamber of scrolls and manuscripts, for instance, which I would have wished to examine more closely. Was this scroll Chinese, or Japanese or Korean? And what did it say, so elegantly, in letters like bees and dragonflies launched across the yellowed sheets, only half unrolled, with faded seals scattered here and there like pressed roses, the insignia of previous owners? Did states, lands, governments exist that produced documents of marriage, property or cases presented in court with such artistry – settlements of wills and disputes, perhaps decrees and laws and declarations of war and peace? What were they? I compared them in my mind to the tattered files that piled up in heaps on my desk, and marvelled. But only insects examined the ones here, eating their way through papery labyrinths, creating intricate tracks before vanishing, leaving behind networks of faint channels the colour of tea, or rust, and small heaps of grey excrement.

Whole worlds were encrypted here and I looked to my guide for elucidation but he only gave a slight shrug as if to say: what does it matter? The young master collected them and that was what made them precious.

And there was still more to see: cases that held all manner of writing materials with inks reduced to powder at the bottom of glass containers, pens and quills no one would ever use again, seals that no longer stamped; a chamber of clocks where no sand seeped through the hourglasses, water had long since evaporated from the clepsydras, bells were stilled, cuckoos silenced, dancing figures paralysed. Time halted, waiting for a magician to start it again.

The sense of futility was underlined by the sounds my footsteps made on the stone flooring. My guide's feet were shod in slippers that only shuffled. We might have been a pair of ghosts from the museum the owner had conjured up in a dream.

My curiosity was now so reduced that, like a fading spectre, it barely existed. I found myself hurrying after my guide, no longer stopping to admire or decipher, wishing only to bring the tour to an end.

But now we came to a halt in the dustiest and shabbiest chamber of all, as if here the voyager's travels were being rounded up and stored away. It held all the appurtenances of travel itself – leather suitcases with peeling labels of famous hotels still clinging to them, railway and shipping timetables decades out of date and obsolete, baskets held together with string, canvas bedrolls with splitting leather straps and rusty buckles, Gladstone bags as cracked and crushed as broken old men, bundles of bus, ferry and railway tickets preserved by an obsessive, entrance tickets to castles, museums, palaces and picture galleries, reminders of experiences that must once have seemed rich and rewarding. On the walls, peeling posters for lands where beaches were golden, palm trees loaded with coconuts, cruise liners afloat on high seas, flags fluttering – their original colours now barely perceptible. On a table in the centre, an antique globe, round as a teapot, with a map on it centuries out of date, showing continents that had shifted or disappeared and oceans that had spread or shrunk, and portraying marine life – spouting whales, flying fish, as well as mythical creatures like sirens and mermaids, all beckoning: come, come see!

Perhaps this had been the restless young man's source of inspiration. As for me, all desire I had ever felt for adventure had been drained away by seeing these traces that he had left of his, this gloomy storehouse of abandoned, disused, decaying objects. Their sad obsolescence cast a spell on me and I wanted only to break free and flee.

But my guide had one more thing he wanted to show me. Pointing at a long, shallow box that stood open along one wall, he said, 'This was the final box we received. It was empty and Srimati Sarita Devi knew it was the last. She said to me, "There will not be another."'

'And there wasn't?' I asked, wondering if I was meant to take this as some miraculous revelation of a mother's bond to her child or if it would lead to another tale.

'No, no more boxes.'

'And did he himself not return?'

He shook his head and, as if to avoid a show of emotion, turned aside and pushed open the last heavy door.

And suddenly we found ourselves expelled from the darkness and gloom and outside on the wide stairs open to the white blaze of day. I tried to adjust my eyes to the harsh contrast and to think of something to say, but my mouth was dry and stale, in need of a drink of water. I turned to my host to take my leave and was startled to find he did not at all intend to let me go. Instead, he was hurrying down the stairs to the dusty, uninviting field below, no longer the meek, obsequious clerk who had come to petition me at the circuit house, nor the proud curator of what he clearly deemed a valuable piece of property, but a small, determined man doggedly performing his duties to the last.

'Where are we going now?' I protested, unwillingly following him to the foot of the stairs.

He turned back, suddenly snapped open an umbrella – a large black dome lifted on its rusty spokes – that he must have picked out of the unlucky elephant's foot without my noticing and said, 'This way, please, this way. I have one last gift to show you,' and holding the clumsy object over my head to provide me with shade, proceeded to cross the field. We came to what was evidently the end of the extensive compound where there was a brick wall – or the remains of one – rising above the top of which I could see a stand of susurrating bamboo bleached by the sun.

He led me through a doorway – it was actually a gap in the wall and doorless – and suddenly we were in the bamboo grove that I had glimpsed from without. Here, in a rustling, crackling bed of dry, sharp-tipped leaves shed by the bamboo stalks, and looming up in the striped shade like a grounded monsoon cloud, restlessly shifting from one padded foot to another as if fretting at its captivity, an elephant stood chained. Its trunk swung downward as if wilted by the heat and gave out long deep sighs that stirred the dust on the ground. Although the animal glanced at us from under lashes like bristles, with small, sharp, canny eyes, it gave no sign of curiosity or alarm. Weariness perhaps, that was all.

A man, bare-bodied, his waist wrapped in a brief, discoloured rag, rose from where he had been squatting in the shade by some buckets and troughs filled with leaves, and came forward to meet us with, I thought, the same weariness as his charge.

To my surprise, my small timid host went up to the great grey wall of the elephant's side and placed his hand on it, proprietorially. The creature stood listless, the merest twitch running through its flank as if it had been bothered by a fly. And there were flies. Also heaps of dung for them to feed on.

The two men spoke to each other in one of the local dialects unknown to me, the one in rags not even troubling to remove the stalk on which he was chewing from his mouth, and the clerk/curator giving him what sounded like instructions. The keeper of the elephant shrugged and said something laconic from the corner of his mouth and scratched the sparse hairs on his chest. He and his charge, the one minute and the other monumental, shared a surprising number of tics and mannerisms.

The clerk/curator turned to me and his elderly face with its white wisp of a beard looked tired and older still than it had earlier seemed.

'She was the last gift Sri Jiban sent his mother. She travelled to us over the border from Burma; it was a long journey by foot and this was her final destination. Her keeper brought us no letter and no explanation except that she was sent us by *him*, and we have had the care of her and the feeding of her ever since. And it is now many years. Srimati Sarita Devi saw to it as long as she had the strength and the means, then left her in my care. She gave me whatever remained in her hands, then departed for Varanasi where she has lived ever since. I did not hear from her again. Perhaps she is no more. She went there, you see, to die.'

I saw that he laid his hand on the great beast's flank with an immense gentleness; it might have been the touch a father bestows on an idiot son, a mad daughter or an invalid wife, gentle and despairing, because she also provided him with the purpose of his life.

'If she lives longer,' he murmured, 'and requires more feeding, I will have to start dismantling the museum, disposing of it piece by piece. It is her only inheritance.'

I had no idea what I should do or say, and stood there in the shade of the monstrous cloud, staring at the flies and the shifting padded feet and the dust they stirred up, away from the two small, spare men who, I now saw, were not only older and shorter than I, but also emaciated, probably lacking even the basic nutrition and necessities, while their ward lived on and on and fed and fed.

Then the clerk put his hands together and turned to me in pleading. 'Sir, please help us. Please appeal on our behalf to the government, the sarkar, to take the museum from us into its custody and provide for us, and for this last gift we were sent. I am ashamed, sir, but I can no longer care for her myself. Forgive me for begging you.'

I could not think of what to say, how to meet his request, his evident need. I mumbled something about it being late, about having to get back, about how I would think about what could be done and how I would let him know as soon, as soon as –

That year of my training in the service is long past. I have been for years now in senior positions, mostly in the capital. I have been transferred from one ministry to another, have dealt with finance, with law and order, with agriculture, with mines and minerals, with health care and education . . . you could call it a long and rewarding career of service. I might even say my father took some pride in it. I am of course no longer the lonely bachelor I was when I was first sent out to the districts and compelled to stay in that benighted circuit house; my mother was able to arrange a marriage for me to a wife who is in every way suited to me and my life, and I am a family man with grown sons and daughters. In fact, I rarely think back to that time now.

I am ashamed to say that once I was transferred to the capital I did not look back, I did not keep in touch with the keeper of the museum and I never found out what happened to it, or to him. What is that saying about ships passing in the night? Is there a landlocked version of it – caravans passing in the desert, or elephants in the forest?

Elephants – now those are creatures which make me uneasy still. Of course I rarely encounter one. Even when my children were young, I avoided zoos, circuses, any place an elephant might be sighted. I feared to have that sad, shrewd eye turned on me, taking my measure and finding it wanting.

Once I had a nightmare – it was while I was still in the district and it was never repeated and never forgotten – in which such a beast devoured, blade by blade, leaf by leaf, an entire forest till it was laid waste, and then it raised its trunk and stepped forward to the tree where I was hiding, to expose – what? I don't know because such nightmares do not have endings. One flees them by waking.

And in wakefulness I would think of the immense creature as innocent and defenceless, who dwindles from neglect and finally lies down not to rise again. A death so huge as to be incomprehensible. This disturbs me and I turn away to distract myself from it. I know behind it is the question: Could I have done more? But it is not for us to do everything for everyone. In the end my reputation in the service was good, solid. What else could I have done?

In fact, by now I am not even sure the museum existed, or the man who created it or his mother who received it or the keeper who kept it. Or if it was a mirage I saw or a book I once read and only vaguely remembered, with none of the solidity, the actuality of objects and men and beasts.

Occasionally a scene from it will rise out of my subconscious just as I am drifting into sleep. Then it slips away.

Translator Translated

THE TWO WOMEN had not met since they were in school together. And at that time they barely had anything to do with each other. That is how it is, of course, when one is a natural-born leader, excels in both sports and studies, is captain of any number of societies, a model for the subdued and discouraged mediocrities who cannot really aspire to imitating her and who feel a disturbing mix of envy and admiration – currents travelling in opposite directions and coiling into treacherous and unsettling whirlpools – and the other, meanwhile, belongs to the latter group, someone who stands out neither by her looks nor her brains and whom others later have a hard time remembering as having been present at all.

Yet, at the Founder's Day function held at their old school one year, they were both present in the small group of alumni who attended. Prema, now middle-aged, even prematurely aged one might say, found herself in the presence of someone she had admired for so long from afar. It would not have occurred to her to approach the tall, elegant woman with a lock of white hair gleaming like a bold statement amid the smooth black tresses that swung about her shoulders. The woman wore enormous dark glasses – they used to be called 'goggles' – which she removed only to read the programme, but she must have looked around her and taken in more because she half turned in her seat to Prema who sat behind her and said, quite naturally and unaffectedly, 'We were in the same class, weren't we? Do you remember?' And Prema had to make a pretence of being puzzled, confused and surprised, before remembering – as if she had ever forgotten.

Prema's astonishment at being recognised made her tongue-tied. As a schoolgirl she had never gone up and spoken to Tara – there had been no occasion to do so. Only once was a connection made, when she threw a ball right across the court with an unaccustomed, even anguished force, and Tara, leaping to catch it, twirled so that her short pleated skirt whipped about her hips, and effortlessly, balletically, lifted the ball into the net to eruptions of cheers. Now Prema could find nothing to say. If only there were, again, a ball to fling and to catch, so gloriously! Finally, 'It's been a long time,' she stammered, and wished she had dressed better and brought her new handbag with her instead of the cloth satchel into which she stuffed books, papers, everything – just the way only the most despised and unfashionable teachers did.

'Not when one is back here – it's changed so little,' Tara said easily. 'Miss Dutt is gone, of course. I wish I'd come sooner and seen her again.'

Miss Dutt, the dragon? She wished she had seen her again?

Prema blinked: it just showed what different worlds th[...]
pied. To Prema, Miss Dutt had never been anything but a s[...]
and a terror; she could still remember the withering stare she
cast at Prema's battered shoes, unshined, slovenly and uncouth.

'One is too busy,' she said finally, awkwardly. 'Where is the
time?'

She should not have said that; it made Tara ask, 'What have
you been doing all these years?' which of course uncovered the
hollowness of Prema's words. What *had* she been doing that she
could talk of, compared with Tara's achievements of which
everyone knew?

Prema had kept herself informed of Tara's career: how could
one not when it had been so much mentioned in the media
– one of the first interns to be taken on by a national paper,
later a contributor to an international magazine, especially
popular in their part of the world, eventually with her own
syndicated column. It had been a bit surprising when she gave
up her career in journalism and took up publishing instead, in
those days not so glamorous as it seemed to have become now.
She had founded the first feminist press in the country and
made it, unexpectedly, an outstanding success. At least once a
week a photograph of her attending a conference or speaking
at a seminar appeared. And how could Tara possibly have kept
herself informed of Prema's progress – or stasis? Naturally there
was no mention of that to be found anywhere.

But now there was a flurry of activity up on the stage,
behind the row of potted palms; while the microphone was

shifted and adjusted, figures came and disappeared, the next item on the programme was revealed to be not quite ready, and Tara actually seemed willing to carry on this pointless conversation that Prema wished she had not begun.

And then a providential act took place. A small, grubby paperback slid out of the overstuffed, ungainly satchel that Prema was trying to keep from falling off her lap. And as Prema tried to stuff it back before any further objects followed it out, Tara, idly continuing the conversation since nothing else seemed to be happening, asked, 'What is that you're reading?'

Prema had to hold it out for her observation so as not to seem unduly secretive, confident that Tara could not read the script in which it was printed, so distant was it from life here in the capital. But, as she did so, the thought flitted across her mind like an unforeseen fly that Tara may be genuinely interested since she was a publisher and in a very specialised field. Prema realised that there was, after all, something about which they might converse.

'It is in Oriya,' she said, handing over the soiled copy and regretting how badly she had used it, dog-earing the pages, scribbling in the margins, even putting down cups of tea on its cover so that the lurid illustration of a forest fire, a burning hut and a fleeing woman was marked with brown rims. 'It is very good,' she hastened to assure Tara in spite of its appearance to the contrary. 'Very moving.'

'Who is it by? And do you read Oriya?'

Prema fussily adjusted the spectacles on the bridge of her

46

nose in an embarrassment grotesquely enlarged by their lenses. 'It was my childhood language. And it is written by a woman who comes from the same area where my mother lived. She is very much respected there even if no one knows about her here.'

Tara continued to hold the book and turn its pages as if they could impart something to her. Onstage a row of school-girls in the school uniform of pleated skirts, white blouses, knitted ties, limp socks and once-white gym shoes had lined up to sing, but the book seemed to interest her more even if she could not read one letter in that script. When the song onstage ended – rising in a crescendo that could not possibly be maintained and wasn't – she handed the book back to Prema, saying, 'I wish I could read it. I am thinking of starting a new division of my publishing house. We've published texts in English, you see, but I want to branch into translations now, and publish writers well known in their own regions but unknown outside which is such a shame. What do you think?'

Inarticulate Prema could not at first reply but her specta-cles glittered with the enthusiasm of her unspoken response until, just before the principal's speech began to be broadcast, the loudspeaker causing it to echo at fluctuating volume, she managed to say, fervently, 'That is a *wonderful* idea. That is what we *need.*'

Then the principal was well launched upon her speech, the microphone tamed, it seemed, by her authority, and there was no alternative but to be silent and listen. At the end of it, some of the women who had been in their class and recognised Tara – although clearly not Prema – swooped upon her with cries and exclamations and Prema picked up her satchel and retreated. It was time for tea.

When she got home on the bus and climbed the stairs to her rooftop apartment – left unswept as usual by the landlady's slatternly maid (she would have to complain again) – the day was sinking into its murky nicotine-tinged haze of dust with home-going traffic pouring through it like blue-black oil from a leak in the street below. The crows that spent the day swinging on the electric and telephone wires and squabbling were dropping into the scraggly branches of the lopped tree below with exhausted squawks. Would she allow herself to be dragged into the gloom by it all once again? Heaving the cloth satchel off her shoulder (which had become permanently lowered by its familiar weight), she determined she would not. Letting spill the book she had shown Tara – which had so miraculously caught Tara's eye – she ran her fingers lightly over its smeared and smudged cover because that was where Tara had thought to run hers, and then opened it out on the table where she worked, ate, wrote and arranged her books, papers and pens. Without even fetching herself a glass of water or sitting down to rest, she read the first few lines to herself and once again the syllables of that language evoked the distant world which linked her to the writer.

It was the place where her father had been posted, briefly,

as a junior officer in government service, and where he had met and married her mother, his landlady's daughter – to the horror and consternation of his family, who had never imagined such a thing as an inter-caste marriage between its strict boundaries, and to the sorrow and foreboding of hers, equally strict within its own limits – then brought her back with him to the city. It was in her earliest years, steadily growing more distant, more remote in its wrappings of nostalgia, that Prema had heard her mother speak to her and sing to her in her language (only when her father was not present; he could not tolerate it once he was back where he belonged, in the capital). But after her mother's early death (hadn't her family foretold it, *exactly* this?) Prema had lost contact with what was literally her mother tongue. Then recovered it by choosing to study the language at an adult education evening class during a slack period in her life, after receiving her degree in English literature, a respectable but common qualification.

Not content to stop there, for some reason she could not explain to her father or his family who considered it an aberration, unfathomable in someone given the opportunity to take up any line of study at any college she chose, she decided it was imperative that she visit the region where Oriya was a spoken, living language. Her teacher, a preternaturally mild and soft-spoken man, dangerously thin and withdrawn, had offered, on hearing her plan, a baffled smile which confirmed that no previous student of his had ever responded in this way to the evening classes he gave so timidly and tentatively, in an almost empty classroom made available in a local, underfunded school for such lost souls as herself. He seemed unsure whether to congratulate her or warn her.

She remembered with what trepidation she had made her travel arrangements – if one could use the term 'arrangement' for such a haphazard journey involving many changes from broad- to narrow-gauge railway, then country buses, finally a choice of horse-drawn tonga or bicycle rickshaw – and how warily she had faced her time in a women's hostel at a local college, no more than a scattering of brick barracks in a dusty field. There was a tea stall under a drooping neem tree where she kept herself alive on tea and biscuits through the many slow, stifling days she had to spend there before the language lifted itself off the pages of her textbook and assumed once again the mobility, the unselfconscious agility it had once had for her. Almost to her surprise, it slowly became recognisable in the speech of the tea-stall owner, the cycle-rickshaw driver and the women in the hostel with whom she shared a bathroom – a row of stalls along a perpetually wet and dripping hall – and whom she ran into after classes were over and there were empty evenings to while away.

Turning the pages of the limp little paperback, running her eyes over the script, she thought with a kind of guilty nostalgia of the homesickness she had suffered for the city, for its comforts and conveniences rather, and how she had found, once she could converse again in their language, that the other women were just as homesick for the villages and hamlets from which they had come for their 'higher education'. They named them to her – she had never even seen them on a map – and she asked questions continually, always picturing her mother, as a girl, living in such a place as they described.

One day, in class, her teacher named this very writer whose book lay open before her – Suvarna Devi – and spoke of her as the unsung heroine of Oriya letters. She told Prema, the most ardent student she had ever had, that it was worth learning the language simply to read the work of Suvarna Devi. 'She will not only reveal the sweetness of the language to you but open your eyes to what you don't even know exists here.' So Prema stopped in the bazaar on her way back to the hostel and found this very paperback amid the magazines, calendars and greeting cards with which the so-called bookshop was mainly stocked. She showed her find to the women at the hostel who expressed amazement that she had not known about this writer: they had been made to read her short stories in school – not always with reverence, it seemed. One of the women who stood out from the others because she wore her hair cropped in a place where all the other women had long pigtails or tightly wound and carefully pinned buns, and even wore trousers if she was not going to classes, said, 'Why do you want to waste your time reading Suvarna Devi? You won't get a job at a university if you do. You need to read Jane Austen, George Eliot and Simone de Beauvoir. No university will look at you if you haven't read *The Second Sex*. Forget Suvarna Devi, read the feminists, read Simone de Beauvoir.' This reduced many of the others to helpless laughter; they tried out the foreign name in many different ways, all of which sounded absurd.

Prema not only read the collection of Suvarna Devi's short stories but returned to the bookshop to see if they had any more of her work. They did not, but in the college library she came across a journal the writer had kept while living in the tribal areas to the south; it was bound in green Rexine and the library flap at the back showed that it had been issued to readers exactly twice in the last seven years. Prema borrowed it and took it back to read in the hostel and found that the journal entries, many of them of an anthropological nature, and the notes on village life in the forest, provided a backdrop for the fiction she had already read but were otherwise disappointingly dry. Prema had little interest in nature or the rituals and ceremonies of tribal society per se and found the notes lacking in the characters and events that had made the short stories so lively and engaging.

She asked her companions at the hostel if they knew anything of the life of this author, so oddly divided between literature and anthropology. 'Oh, she goes to those areas with her husband,' they told her. 'He is a doctor and runs clinics there. Who wants to read about *that*?' It suddenly occurred to Prema that the writer might live in this very town. She was told, casually, that yes, they believed she did. 'Where?' cried Prema. 'Can you tell me *where*?' Her mind leapt ahead to that prized objective of any serious student: a personal interview. Besides, such a meeting might create another link to her mother's world. And there was so little time left, she was due to return to Delhi in just a week. Someone told her in which part of the town Suvarna Devi's husband had his practice but no one could give her a specific address. They knew Suvarna Devi's work from their school syllabus but that did not make her a local celebrity: instead, it just made her one of them.

Prema went there on foot one day, after her class, to see if she could find it for herself. It was a neighbourhood rather like a suburb on the far outskirts of Delhi where the city petered out into the dusty plains, a jumble of small bungalows no longer new, many with signboards on their gates to denote their middle-class status: doctors, lawyers, advocates, specialists in gynaecology, homeopathy, ayurveda, urology, and also schools that gave evening classes in typing, shorthand and tailoring.

Not knowing the exact address and coming across the same surnames repeated over and over, Prema gave up, suddenly conscious of the dust gathering between her toes and invading the folds of her neck and elbows, sticky and gritty at the same time. She could not continue to trail up and down the maze of little streets with dogs barking at her through closed gates, men staring at her from bicycle and radio repair shops and concrete bus shelters under stunted, lopped trees. Defeated, she returned to the hostel.

It did not matter, she told herself as she packed for the long journey back to the capital; she had found the subject of her studies and that was all that mattered. How could she have returned *without* one?

Her thesis supervisor accepted the subject with the greatest reluctance: it was not part of the regular syllabus and it was hard to see how it could be made to fit in. But then Prema showed she could be stubborn when she chose: her subject was not the language itself but the author and how her work belonged to the greater world. She wrote the thesis and, rather to her supervisor's surprise, it was accepted.

She might have anticipated what followed. After so many years of thinking this would be the climax of her life, she discovered that instead everyone expected her to continue as if there had been no such climax. What next? she was asked continually, by family and friends, what next?

After a wait of too many unhappy and discouraging years – the first sighting of stray white hairs a defining moment – she finally accepted a junior position in a minor women's college in a bleak and distant quarter of the city. And even here her thesis counted for little. What an odd subject, they all thought, a writer in Oriya? Why, what had made her pursue such an unpromising course of study? Why had she not gone to Jawaharlal Nehru University and studied French, Russian or Chinese? What good was this provincial author in a provincial language to her or to anyone here? So Prema found herself in the department of English literature after all, teaching Jane Austen and George Eliot (though not Simone de Beauvoir).

This left a small, smouldering ember deep inside her soul (so she designated its location, no other would do), where it released an odour of heated rubber, threatening to destroy whatever pleasure or satisfaction she might court. It burnt two deep grooves across her forehead as if with a stick of charcoal, and two more from the corners of her nostrils to the edges of her mouth. Sometimes, when passing a shop window filled with spangled and sequinned saris that encouraged reflection, or catching a glimpse of herself in the small, chipped mirror over her bathroom sink, she was startled by the grimness of her expression. No wonder she was rarely invited out, or made part of any gathering for celebration or enjoyment. She turned away and trudged along to the bus stop with the satchel of books weighing down her left shoulder. She put in the necessary hours of work, meeting her colleagues in the staffroom during the lunch hour which they all utilised to complain of their workload and the perfidy of the principal and heads of departments, and the disrespectful, boisterous and unruly students. At the end of the day she trudged back even more depressed than when she had set out. That was when she wondered if her life was any different from that of the crows dividing their time between the telephone lines and the dying tree in her street with equally raucous disorder and dissent.

This was what had made her accept the invitation to attend the Founder's Day function at her old school. Her schooldays had not been a particularly happy period in her life either – she had already shown signs of a failed life there, it seemed, something that attracts no friends – but at least it was now so far back in the past that she could look back on it forgivingly, almost benignly.

And, as it happened, it had turned out well. She had not only met her old school idol Tara, after so many years of following her brilliant career in the press, but Tara had recognised *her*, and by showing an interest in the book that had so providentially fallen out of her satchel, given her a nod.

A nod. Such a small gesture, almost inconspicuous, but it was what Prema had been waiting for, she now realised, a nod no one had been willing to give her before. It must have been the sign she needed because now, sitting over the empty plate from which she had eaten her dinner – some slices of bread with pickles – the book propped up beside the pickle jar, the sugar pot and the bottle of antacid pills, she began to have thoughts that ought to have come to her earlier: thoughts, plans, like a hand of cards dealt to her that were worth studying.

She began nodding to herself, unconsciously but encouragingly. In the street below, quieter now than an hour or two earlier, a car with a siren tore past, screeching its metallic nail across her eardrum. But Prema barely noticed, even though it set all the neighbourhood dogs howling.

Having made an appointment – costing her an anguish of indecision no one else would have understood – Prema was at Tara's office in Sri Aurobindo Market punctually at three o'clock on a Friday afternoon. She was somewhat disappointed to find Tara's office was not in a shiny new high-rise but in somewhat obscure quarters above a grimy copy shop with a small arrow on the wall pointing up the stairs, stairs just as unswept as in her own building, she noted. The office itself, she was relieved to find, was bright and neat, freshly painted, with a tall potted plant in the corner that appeared to be flourishing, and a row of shelves on which the latest publications of Tara's press were lined up, the newest of them facing out. These were so attractive – small in size but with covers of terracotta, lapis lazuli and moss green, each with a small miniature painting printed in the centre above the title and below the author's name – that Prema felt deeply ashamed of the state of the paperback she had brought with her to refresh Tara's memory. While the secretary dialled Tara's number to announce the visitor, Prema gazed at these delectable, desirable objects, recognising some of the authors' names and wondering about the others. Then the door opened and there was Tara, dark glasses pushed back over her hair, which Prema now saw had a fashionable red glow of henna, and wearing a sari that was elegant in its extreme simplicity – fine white cotton, black-bordered, such as Prema would never have considered wearing. She looked a bit preoccupied but remembered having made the appointment – flattering in itself – and had Prema come into her office which was larger and untidier than the little reception room, with ceramic coffee mugs amid the books on her desk, and a lingering odour of cigarette smoke.

'It was wonderful to see you the other day,' Prema began, determinedly smiling to keep those depressing wrinkles away, but, on seeing Tara assume a somewhat impatient air, decided to hurry along to the purpose of her visit. Placing the book she had brought with her on the desk between them, she went

on: 'When you said you were thinking of commissioning translations from indigenous languages – our many great languages
– and bringing writers to the notice of those readers who don't
know them – I thought of Suvarna Devi.' She had to stop for
breath, she had spoken so fast and was almost panting. 'She is
such a great writer and no one here even knows her name. It
is very sad but I am sure if you publish a translation of her
work, she will become as well-known as – as – Simone de
Beauvoir,' she ended in an inspired burst.

Tara was listening, although she was playing with a pencil
and occasionally glancing at her watch – she clearly had something on her mind, probably another engagement coming up
– but after calling her secretary to send in a bottle of Fanta for
Prema – such a hot day – she did begin to tell Prema her plan
for this new division of her publishing house and what she
hoped to publish under its imprint. 'Of course, I am no linguist
myself,' she apologised, 'and I will have to depend on others –
academics and critics – to tell me what they think worthwhile.'

And by the time the Fanta had been drunk (bringing on
an embarrassing sequence of barely suppressed burps) and Prema,
the academic and critic, was on her way out, it had been decided
she would write a synopsis of the book, a brief biography and
bibliography of Suvarna Devi's work, and a few pages – oh, five
or ten – of her translation as a sample. Once she had sent that
in, she would hear from Tara. Yes, definitely, within a month –
or two at the most.

Then the secretary rang to announce the next visitor and

Tara flew out of her chair to receive the young man who had come in with his arms flung wide, no longer merely polite but positively exuberant. Of course, he *was* young and attractive, Prema could see that before she left.

What actually saddened me when I left was not the sight of masculine youth and its attraction for Tara but the thought, now settling on me as I sat on the bus – it was a Ladies' Special which was why I had a seat – that Tara had not asked me a single question about my involvement with this language. I had been given no opportunity to explain how I came about it, what it meant to me and why, while teaching the usual, accepted course of English literature in a women's college, I had maintained my commitment to it. I could have told her so much, so much – but was given no chance and so I had to keep the information withheld, a secret. No one knew what a weight that exerted, one I longed to relieve.

But, getting off the bus and climbing the stairs to my room at the top, I found I could, in a quite miraculous way, unload myself of that weight. As soon as I took out the little paperback – its pages were coming loose from the binding, I noticed – and pulled a piece of paper to me and began to translate the first line, it was as if I had been given a magic key that would open the rest.

'*It started to rain. It was getting dark.*'

But no – immediately I could see how blunt that looked, how lacking in spirit. Where was the music, the lilt of the original?

'Rain began to fall. The village was in darkness.'

Yes, and yes. How easy to see that these words worked, the others did not. I hurried on, hurried while that sense lasted of what was right, what was wrong, an instinct some-times elusive which had to be courted and kept alert. Selecting, recognising, acknowledging. I was only the conduit, the medium between that language and this – but I was the one doing the selecting, the discriminating, and I was the only one who could; the writer herself could not. I was inter-preting the text for her because I had the power – too strong a word perhaps, but the ability, yes. I was also the one who knew what she meant, what worlds her words evoked. They were not mine but they were my mother's. I barely remem-bered her or those earliest years spent in her lap; I only imag-ined I did. I was not sure if I had ever seen the shefali tree's night-blooming flowers in the morning, or the pond where blue lotuses bloomed and intoxicated bumblebees buzzed, or heard the sound of cattle lowing as they made their way homewards at twilight, but at some subconscious level, I found I knew them just as she did. Translating Suvarna Devi's words and text into English was not so different, I thought, from what she herself must have felt when writing them in her own language, which was, after all, a kind of translation too – from seeing and hearing and feeling into syntax. And I, who had inherited the language, understood it and under-stood her in a way no one else could have done, by instinct and empathy. The act of translation brought us together as if we were sisters – or even as if we were one, two compatible halves of one writer.

Of course there were instances – small stumbles – when I could not find the exact word or phrase. In Suvarna Devi's language, each word conjured a whole world; the English equivalent, I had to admit, did not. Cloud, thunder, rain. Forest and pool. Rooster and calf. How limited they sounded if they could not evoke the scene, its sounds and scents – images without shadows. Perhaps an adjective was needed. Or two, or three.

I tried them out. In the original, adjectives were barely used, but I needed them to make up for what was lost in the translation. Of course I could see that restraint was called for, I had to hold fast. Not too fast, though. A middle way. A golden mean.

I laughed out loud and struck my forehead with my hand to think of all the different strains and currents of my life and how they were coming into play. I had never felt such power, never *had* such power, such joy in power. Or such confusion.

I stopped only when I became aware it was night outside, the crows silent, the street lights burning, the traffic thinning, its roar subsiding into a tired growl. The television set in my landlady's flat was turned on, the evening soap opera at full volume – and I hadn't even noticed it earlier.

Pushing back my hair – as if I too had a pair of dark glasses perched up there, or a gleaming strand of distinguished white like Tara! – I got up, picked up my purse, went downstairs and crossed the street to the small shop where I sometimes bought essentials, a bar of soap or a packet of candles during a power breakdown. Tonight, though, I bought a packet of cigarettes – not the brand I had seen on Tara's desk and that I wanted but a cheaper one that the shopkeeper stocked. I had never bought cigarettes from him before and he gave me a strange look. He recognised me of course but I didn't care what he thought. This was something I was now discovering – that there were things about which I did not need to care. I recrossed the street with the packet in my purse, stepping aside just in time to avoid an autorickshaw that came careering round the corner, its driver singing at the top of his lungs with the joy of going home, free, at the end of a day's work. I almost could not restrain an impulse to join in before I went up the stairs to my room to see what the cigarettes could do for me, for my new career – Prema Joshi, translator.

Smoking one was another matter, I admit, and not very successful. I was glad no one was there to observe how I doubled over, coughing, and stubbed out the obnoxious weed, in disappointment.

The synopsis and the sample pages were quickly done. Perhaps a little too quickly, Prema worried, but found she really did not wish anything to slow or halt the momentum, and so she slipped them into a brown paper envelope and took them to be posted in the same flush of high excitement with which she had written them.

Tara had her secretary call Prema – that was a disappointment, Prema had not expected to have to deal with an intermediary – to tell her to go ahead with the translation. So the first step had been taken, and Prema drew a deep breath, poised now on the brink of this new career.

Her old career began to seem irksome. Her lectures became perfunctory; she no longer cared if they did not inspire her students with the same passion she felt for literature. *The Mill on the Floss*, *Emma*, *Persuasion* – what did they mean to these girls? She marked their papers impatiently, merely skimming them, not stopping to put right their grotesque errors and misrepresentations. She could not be bothered: every one of these girls would leave college to marry, bear children and, to everyone's huge relief, never read another book.

All that mattered now was to do as fine a translation as possible of Suvarna Devi's stories, so simple in their language and structure, but how forceful and powerful for all that!

The experience had aspects to it that Prema had not imagined when she set out. It reminded her, for instance, of how she had struggled to write stories herself when she was young – younger – and how she had sent them out to magazines only to have them returned with curt rejection slips, the hurt and bitterness with which she had mourned them as she put them away, and how discouragement had made her admit she was probably no writer after all.

Now she could laugh at those rejections and the way she had taken them to heart, letting their poison seep into her till the urge to write, the ambition to write, had quite died inside her.

She realised that all she had needed was this opportunity, this invitation held out to her – by Tara, of all people – to discover her true vocation. It was surely the right one since it had given her this new-found ease, and speed, and delight.

So the work was done sooner than she, and perhaps Tara, had expected, and it was with a certain sense of regret, and trepidation, that she typed it out, then had a typist she knew at a copy shop down the road retype it for neatness – 'Don't worry, auntie,' he said, 'it will look just like print' – and carried the bundle ceremoniously to Tara's office. Mailing it was of course possible and perhaps more professional but she couldn't resist the satisfaction of handing it over herself and seeing Tara's face register approval. The completion of this labour needed somehow to be marked and rewarded.

Unfortunately, Tara was away. Her secretary informed Prema that she was at a conference in Prague, would be back in a week. If she left the manuscript, it would be given to Tara on her return. Prema could expect to hear from her very soon.

She did not. Tara took her time, a very long time it seemed to Prema. In fact, Prema advanced from disappointment to impatience to annoyance at being treated in this manner and kept waiting as if she were only one of many people in a queue for Tara's attention. Had she no consideration for what an author – all right, a translator – might feel at being ignored, left in the dark, waiting, hoping?

She could feel the grooves across her forehead and from her

nostrils to her mouth deepening by the day. She snapped at her students. She marked their papers with increasing severity. She knew they found her unfair, ill-tempered and dull. But why did they consider themselves worthy of her attention? They were not, not. She was a translator, an author.

Then, just like that, a change in the atmosphere, a sudden breeze to fill her sails, give her hope and move her forwards at last.

A telephone call from Tara – first her secretary, then Tara herself – to say she was pleased, she approved the translation and would publish it; it would appear in the first list of translations by her press.

It was true she did not exactly convey enthusiasm. She was certainly not effusive. In fact she did not even say she thought the translation 'good'. She said it was 'quite good'. Could there be a more tepid qualification?

That might have crushed Prema as much as an outright rejection but Tara followed that limp opinion by saying she would get in touch with Suvarna Devi to draw up a contract, and asked if Prema knew how she might do that.

So suddenly Prema had not only to see to the few notes and suggestions Tara made about the translation – just as the students were sitting their exams which meant their papers would soon be pouring in for her to mark – but she also had to busy herself with finding out about Suvarna Devi's whereabouts. *Why* had she not done that when she was actually there in her home town? And why did the publisher of her book, evidently a local one in the same town, not reply to her queries?

It all proved incredibly difficult and frustrating. Until she thought of writing to the principal of the women's college where she had spent that one summer. To that she received a reply with an address but also a warning that she was often away in the tribal regions with her husband who ran a string of clinics there (and where she obviously found the material for those heartbreaking stories that Prema found so moving).

Weeks went by without a response to Prema's letter in which she had introduced herself and informed her of Tara's publishing house and its new imprint. Would their proposal to publish her short stories meet with her approval?

There was a long stretch, a very long stretch, of waiting again and Prema found it hard to maintain her hope of a new career in the face of such silence. She tried to be patient, telling herself that the mail in those jungle outposts had to be slow and unreliable, but at the same time she felt that a matter of such importance *ought* to break through and elicit a reply.

Eventually it did – a letter written on several small sheets of yellow stationery, each sheet with a red rose printed in the top corner, the stationery of someone who was not accustomed to writing letters except on special occasions requiring a rose. Prema was both touched and a little apprehensive: it did not denote professionalism.

Still, she took it across to Tara in a state of some excitement and translated the few lines expressing thanks for the interest shown in her 'humble work'. Tara wondered how to draw up a contract with someone who might not be able to read it but Prema assured her it was quite possible that she did – after all, she *was* a published writer – and besides, her husband who was a doctor would surely be able to go over it with her. Tara was encouraged to proceed.

Happy times followed for Prema – feeling free to visit Tara's office, sharing her editorial notes with her, going over them together, discussing such matters as footnotes and glossaries, then seeing through the galleys and the proofs, picking the right illustration for the forest-green cover they chose, and the artistic lettering to go with it – roman of course but with Sanskritic embellishment.

Prema brimmed over and shone, gleamed as never before. Tara began to search for other titles to publish under the new imprint. Sometimes Prema was included when she discussed another literary gem she had discovered or consulted regarding a suitable translator. Prema became so light-hearted, she smiled and laughed even with her students who began to speculate as to whether she had a lover. The idea made them sputter with laughter, it was so ridiculous, and Prema occasionally caught them at it and felt a twist of suspicion.

Then, through her new contact with the publishing world, she learned there was to be a conference of writers in the 'indigenous languages' who had no outlet to the larger market and a wider readership.

'Tara,' she found herself saying with a new-found confidence and optimism that made her push back the (invisible) white strand in her hair and the non-existent dark designer glasses, 'we must make sure Suvarna Devi is invited to attend!'

The publication of her book was hurried along so that it could be brought out in time for the conference. Prema could think of nothing else – college, students, exams, all receded page by page, face by face, into a blur in the distance. The central place in her mind was occupied by the beautiful little moss-green book with the Kangra painting of a forest glade on the cover and Suvarna Devi's name in elegantly Sanskritised roman letters. The young man who had burst into Tara's office at their first meeting was the 'genius' behind the design. Inside were the words: *Translated by Prema Joshi*, not in the same painterly script but in print nevertheless, black on white, irrefutable.

When she arrived at the convention hall which was hung with purple and orange bunting for the occasion, Prema went straight to the stall set up in the foyer for the books by authors who had come from all over India for the conference, almost trembling with the anticipation of seeing the book she – well, she together with Suvarna Devi – had created.

Surely this was the crowning moment of her life even if there were no golden bugles to proclaim it. She had prepared for it as nervously as if for a party. Taken out a sari she had bought to wear to the wedding of a young cousin but never worn since; it had a broad red border with a gold trim and was certainly an assertion in itself. But, on putting it on, draping it carefully fold by fold around her middle, she became bitterly critical of the foolishness of dressing up, and changed it for everyday garb. This made her late. She arrived at the convention hall in a fluster with no time to comb her hair, and rushed straight to the bookstall. Her eyesight blurred for an instant as it alighted on the book but that may have been because it was somewhat obscured by other titles in bigger letters, on brighter, glossier and, she thought, rather vulgar covers. After taking in this slight, Prema reached out surreptitiously and quickly reordered the books so that Suvarna Devi's lay on top, others beneath, then moved on: the conference was due to be inaugurated by the Minister of Education, and all were requested to be in their seats before he entered with his entourage.

The loudspeaker whined excruciatingly. Then sputtered, then brayed. Harassed men ran around trying to fix it, alternately shouting 'Stop, stop' and 'OK, go'. The minister slumped into his chair, looking disgusted. The 'honoured guests' who occupied the front rows sat very stiff and upright, waiting for things to be fixed and proceedings to start. Prema found herself embarrassed that things were not going more smoothly but of course this was how all such affairs began, and probably in the regions from which the writers came things were no different.

Eventually the minister made his speech. He read it slowly – as if he did not think the honoured guests, representing so many different languages, could possibly follow, or perhaps he just was and always had been a slow reader (the speech was, after all, written for him by someone else). Then a younger man, perhaps a junior minister, spoke, very rapidly so as to get the greatest number of words into the allotted time – which still seemed to most of the audience far too long. Everyone had come not to hear the bureaucrats but the authors after all, and most of them had travelled a great distance to come to the capital, bringing papers to read which they had written themselves. They were staying at various government hostels scattered about the city and had come together for the first time with much to say for themselves and to each other.

Prema, seated further back, stared at the backs of their heads, wondering which one belonged to Suvarna Devi, her protégée, as she thought of her fondly, protectively. But there were quite a few women among the delegates, none of whom Prema knew by sight. She had to wait till the official speeches were over, the minister escorted out into the foyer, to prowl among the delegates and try to guess who was hers – *her* trophy.

She had never seen a photograph of Suvarna Devi, had been told she was reclusive, that she rarely left her home town and environs, and that was all. So Prema searched the outer edges of the crowd which was made up of the more social and animated delegates of whom there were many. In fact, the roar of voices was rising rapidly into the great pink sandstone cupola above them till it was interrupted by an announcement: the conference would now continue.

If anyone was interested in the spectrum of languages in India, this was certainly the place to be – the place, the day and the time. One after the other the delegates stepped up to the podium to be met by the applause of their particular, and separate, readers, editors and publishers. Bengalis in the audience applauded the Bengali author, Gujaratis the Gujarati, Punjabis the Punjabi and so on. To begin with, the simultaneous translators tried valiantly to keep up with the babel, then faltered, then fell aside.

Providentially a lunch break was announced, when everyone could assemble in the foyer once again, to lift the lids off great serving dishes of stainless steel and dip into bubbling and aromatic concoctions, then go on to little glass dishes of syrupy sweets.

It was very late in the long day when finally Suvarna Devi's name was announced as the next speaker. By then many delegates had visibly succumbed to the soporific effects of the large meal and the warm afternoon.

Suvarna Devi too seemed tired by the proceedings that had gone before. That was Prema's first impression – how tired she seemed, how apart from the rest of the pleased, satisfied crowd. Wrapped about in her grey cotton sari and wearing a shawl that was clearly a sample of her region's weaving, incongruously bright, and steel-rimmed spectacles perched on her nose, in a small, hurried voice she spoke a few lines in the language she wrote in but which only a segment of the audience understood.

Of course Prema did. And Prema, after an initial disappointment at how unimpressive, how unprepossessing a figure her writer cut on the stage during her five minutes of public fame – she would have liked her to be more assured, more flamboyant, more like Tara, she admitted – began to feel an unaccustomed urge to take this elderly, unassuming woman under her wing, protect her and support her as she might a sister or an elder. She hardly paid attention to the speech, so involved was she in taking in Suvarna Devi's presence, trying to connect it to her writing, out of which she had constructed an image that was not quite corroborated by the reality.

Then the proceedings for the day were over and everyone poured out of the auditorium into the foyer. Prema went scurrying around agitatedly like a beetle ahead of a broom, trying to find her author and have at least one private moment, or two, with her. When she finally found her, she was in conversation with Tara who had managed to locate her and welcome her before Prema could do so. This was upsetting; Prema was upset. Was she not the one to have a word with the author she had discovered and come to know so well during the arduous labour of going over, line by line and word by word, the author's work in a way no one else could claim to have done?

And there was the shy grey person she had hurried to protect and chaperone, conversing with Tara who did not know a word of the language she wrote in and would never have heard of it if it had not been for Prema who now broke in with a cry: 'Suvarna Devi! Oh, at last we meet!'

Suvarna Devi, a little startled, looked from her to Tara. It was Tara who introduced them, formally, instead of the other way round as Prema had imagined the introduction.

'Prema Joshi, your translator, and we hope you are pleased with her –'

Hope? That was all Tara felt, *hope*? Prema found she could barely speak for outrage. She hardly knew how to place herself, how to draw away Suvarna Devi's attention and make Tara leave them alone to discuss what they had in common, author and translator, sisters in spirit.

It looked as if the moment would elude her and the author vanish with barely a word of recognition of who and what her translator represented. She had already folded her hands and bowed, turning away to leave, when Prema flew after her, confronted her and insisted they have a few moments together, to discuss – didn't she know there were matters to discuss?

Suvarna Devi seemed taken aback. Perhaps she had not realised how large a role Prema had played in getting her book accepted by Tara's firm, in making her book available to a larger audience by translating it into English. She seemed like a creature who had been startled out of her forest hiding, one of those well-camouflaged speckled birds that will dart under the bushes on being surprised, and now she was flustered, at a loss as to how to respond. But once Prema had made clear the need to meet again, in private, and talk, she asked Prema to come and see her – if she wished, if she could, if it was not too much trouble, in which case she would quite understand and write a letter instead – at her nephew's house where she was staying. And now she had to go . . . There he was, come to collect her in his car.

It was not what Prema would have planned – in place of a meeting with the author alone so they might have an intellectual discussion about books, translation and language. Suvarna Devi's family – the nephew, a young married man and a dentist, his wife, his little daughter and baby son, his wife's parents, all seated on the veranda of their small house in one of Delhi's outer colonies, having tea together, did everything they could to make Prema feel welcome. Suvarna Devi herself seemed entirely relaxed and happy in their midst, quite unlike her shy, apprehensive public persona the day before.

The nephew, a rotund and affable young man, seemed the most at ease, conversing with Prema in English, asking her about the college where she taught, in between popping a biscuit in the baby's rubbery mouth, then turning to some family gossip with Suvarna Devi in their own language. 'She has never been to visit us before,' he told Prema. 'This is a rare occasion for us. I used to live in her house when I was a schoolboy – there was no school in my village, you see – but since coming to Delhi I have only been back a few times. So now she has to give me all the news from there.' This made Prema feel uneasy and an intruder, in spite of being plied with cups of tea and plates of fried snacks by his wife and her parents. She wondered how long she could behave politely in the circumstances. (It was a long time since she had lived with a family, after all; not since her father had remarried.)

It was only when Suvarna Devi rose to her feet and accompanied Prema down the short drive to the gate where her autorickshaw stood waiting (its driver, asleep on the back seat, having to be woken) that she was able to put some of the questions she had come to ask, at least the most urgent ones.

'Now that the short stories have been published – I hope you liked the translation?' she felt compelled to say, rather desperately.

'Yes, yes, very much, very much,' cooed the woodland bird, soothingly.

That was disappointingly vague, but Prema pursued. 'What do you suggest we do next? Are you working on anything new?'

Suvarna Devi did not seem to have given that any thought. Just as clearly, she had had no discussion with Tara on the future of her writing. She seemed genuinely confused and only on lifting the latch of the gate to let Prema out, she admitted, 'Maybe I will write a novel next, I am thinking about it,' and gave an uncertain laugh at her own temerity.

'You are?' Prema cried with enthusiasm, partly sincere and partly affected to encourage the reluctant author. 'Please send it to me, as soon as you have anything to show. That way I could start work on it immediately. Tara will be so happy to hear of it. Just send me a chapter, or even a few pages at a time, it doesn't have to be the complete work.'

But the shy bird had withdrawn again. She looked almost

afraid as she folded her hands to say goodbye, murmuring, 'I will, I will try,' before she hurried back up the drive to the family on the broad, sheltered and hospitable veranda again.

Prema has barely got home – discarding her satchel, pouring herself a glass of water – when the telephone rings. It is Tara, to inform her that the Association of Publishers has called for a press conference as a coda to the writers' conference.

In a panic, Prema: 'A press conference? What is that?'

She will find out, Tara suggests tersely. 'Be there.'

It is too much, coming so hard on the heels of the conference and the meeting with Suvarna Devi, too much at once. She would like to have a little time to sort it all out before she goes on. She can barely eat or sleep that night, fretting till it is time to leave for the venue.

With almost no transition, it seems, there she is, tired from the sleepless night, on a podium with Tara and people she assumes are publishers and translators too, inquisitorial lights shining into her eyes, making her flinch and blink. For a while she is so discomfited that she can barely pay attention to what is being said or by whom. She is still fidgeting with her papers, her books, adjusting to what she finds is literally a spotlight when, far too soon, the dread moment of interrogation arrives.

A pudgy man in a sweat-stained shirt is standing up somewhere in the hall, holding a microphone and saying, 'I would like to address my question to Prema Joshi, translator of Suvarna Devi's stories.'

Sitting up, tight as tight with fright, out comes a croak: 'Ye–es?'

'What made you decide to translate these stories into a colonial language that was responsible for destroying the original langauge?'

Blank, blank, blank.

Then, blinking, and under an expectant stare from Tara, she stammers out the words, 'But the stories – the stories prove – don't they? – it is not destroyed. It exists.'

A flash from Tara's dark glasses, approving, encouraging. So Prema goes on: 'And isn't the translation – the publication of the translation – a way of preventing it from – ah, loss? And proving it exists to, to – the public?'

'What public are you addressing?' The pudgy man adopts a more belligerent tone now that he has found the person at whom he can direct it. 'The English-speaking world?' he asks rhetorically. 'The international public? Why? Doesn't it already have a readership here?'

'Isn't it – isn't it important,' Prema flusters on as if she were one of her own students being interrogated, 'to make it more widely known?'

'To whom is it important? To the writer? To the reader? To what readers? Here in Hindustan? Or in the West? Employing a Western language indicates your wish to win a Western audience, does it not?'

Tara, sitting forward, tapping impatiently on the tabletop: 'I would like to inform you that a press such as mine –'

Prema sits back in relief, letting Tara take over.

'– aims to reveal the writer to a wider public here in India too. Writing that so far has not been accessible to them. Because I, and my colleagues, believe it is our mission –'

'Ha!' the pudgy man explodes with sarcasm. Now that he is on his feet, with a captive microphone, nothing will make him give it up or sit down. 'Who needs to have this revealed to them? The *English* speakers in this country? Why? Why are you catering to *them*? Why not to the speakers of the many native languages of our country?'

Laughter and applause, both approving.

Tara, very upright and fierce: 'If there are publishers in those languages willing to commission translations, as I have done into English, where are they and why are they not coming forward? They are needed, certainly.' Looking around with raised eyebrows, arousing approving murmurs, she repeats, 'Where are they?'

Prema, in gratitude, turning to convey her appreciation to Tara. Argument has erupted. Terms proliferate that indicate the large number of academics in the audience: Subaltern. Discourse. Reify. Validate.

Prema crouches low, fearing some of them will be flung at her. Wasn't 'subaltern' a military term? She feels like the lowliest of students in her class instead of its leader and hopes none of them is present to observe her shame. Where has she been all this time, reading Jane Austen with them, and George Eliot? What has she been doing, talking of Victorian England and its mores? What has stalled her and kept her from joining the current that is now surging past, leaving her helplessly clinging to the raft of *The Mill on the Floss*, the rock of *Pride and Prejudice*?

The chapters of the promised novel began to come in during the course of that summer, in large Manila envelopes that were always torn around the edges and had to be held together with string. They looked as if they had travelled a long and dusty road and suffered many misadventures along the way – and they probably had. At first I fell upon them as soon as I returned from work and found them lying upon the doormat, then immediately settled down to read them. But quite soon I found myself disappointed and dismayed by what I read.

Instead of the artless charm and the liveliness of the short stories, the novel seemed by contrast slow, almost sluggish, as it followed the fortunes of one family from grandparents to parents to children in a not very interesting town – in fact, very like the dusty, ramshackle one where I had first come across Suvarna Devi's work. I found myself growing increasingly impatient with the noble, suffering grandparents, the quarrelling parents, the drifting children, all of whom seemed to follow predictable paths under the effects of changing circumstances: an increase in wealth followed by a dispersal of property, higher education foundering in lost opportunities – and *too* many births, marriages and deaths. Stories recounted, time and time again, in different ways, all over the world.

Perhaps Suvarna Devi did not read very much herself, and was unaware of that? Or had her work actually deteriorated? Where was the passion and the drama of those early stories? Where was that keen observation that had given them their authenticity?

Instead of the ardent admiration I had felt once for the author, the excited joy with which I had set to work rendering my childhood language as faithfully as possible into English, I now looked on Suvarna Devi's work with a much colder eye. More professional perhaps.

I began to wonder if publishing such a disappointing novel would be good for Suvarna Devi's reputation, which I had worked hard to establish. And what would it do to my newly created career as a translator? That too had to be considered, did it not? Having linked myself to the author, didn't it require the best from both of us? And what about the reputation of Tara's press and this imprint she had introduced with Suvarna Devi's short story collection as its first publication? All these factors had to be considered.

Prema took the manuscript across to Tara. Of course Tara could not read the language and would not be able to judge it till it was translated, but Prema felt compelled to warn her that this was not the masterpiece for which they had hoped. Yet she could not let Tara withdraw from the project and bring her new-found vocation to a halt. The warning would have to be delicately phrased, Tara's interest in it kept alive but no false hopes raised.

Fortunately or not, Tara was distracted and did not seem too concerned by what Prema had to tell her. 'I trust you, Prema,' she said, without too much emphasis. 'I know I can rely on you. Not like the translator of this Urdu novel I was pinning my hopes on. It's a major novel by a brilliant new writer, and the first chapters the translator sent in were wonderful. But now he's gone off to Beirut, never answers letters, just makes promises over the phone and never keeps them. I am *so* annoyed. I was going to give it special treatment.' She tapped the Urdu book on her desk with a pencil impatiently, then glanced at the manuscript Prema had brought in without much interest. '*You* are such a relief,' she sighed. 'I know I can trust you to do your job. It's OK to take your time, no need to hurry.'

Prema bridled, thinking: all this pandering to the Muslim minority, hadn't it gone too far? Really, Tara seemed not to have taken in any of Prema's cautiously worded assessment of Suvarna Devi's novel − as if it didn't matter.

So she picked up the manuscript and carried it away with an aggrieved determination to make of it something Tara *would* notice.

The next step was to make room for the task by taking leave from her college. The principal barely reacted and the students saw her off with undisguised joy: they had been told the substitute would be a Miss Batra, who was known to be younger and livelier, dressed in jeans, was seen to smoke, and intended to introduce them to contemporary American authors not yet admitted to the academic pantheon.

Through the suppurating heat of June and July, under a slowly revolving electric fan, and with perspiration streaming down her face in sheets, Prema settled to trying to rediscover the joy she had initially taken in translation. She suffered from a sense that she was struggling, like a drowning fly, to raise herself up from the dull, turgid prose before her and somehow recover the art of flying.

I knew this was the hardest task I had set myself, the greatest challenge (aside from my initial decision to make this language my field of study). I felt a pressure settle upon my head that was uncomfortable but somehow not suffocating. In fact, the challenge was like a terrific headache that might leave one dazed but also uplifted.

A faithful translation would clearly make for a flat, boring read. I saw that what was needed was for me to be inventive, take things into my own hands and create a style for the book. So, instead of a literal translation, I decided to take liberties with the text – to begin with, Suvarna Devi's modest syntax. And once I did that, I began to enjoy myself. What a difference it made when I turned 'red' to 'crimson', 'anger' to 'rage'. My pen began to fly. Using Suvarna Devi's text as a basis on which to build, I found I could touch it with small brush strokes of colour and variation. Wasn't this what the Impressionist painters had done in those early adventurous days, breaking up flat surfaces to refract light into many scattered molecules, and so reconstruct the surface and make it stir to life?

And together with this 'enhancement', as I named it, of the text, I could see that reduction and deletion were called for too. I had to be a teacher and a critic, underline words she had used again and again: how often could I let her use the same adjective for one character? There was no need to repeat 'gentle' and 'kind-hearted' every time the grandmother was mentioned: her words and acts alone could convey that. And it was not necessary to keep calling the daughter-in-law 'greedy' and 'bad-tempered' if there were incidents that showed her greed and insolence.

As with adjectives, I found verbs and adverbs, too, could go. The death of the grandfather, for instance, described by one character in chapter two, surely did not need to be repeated in chapter three by another character with the same 'wailing' and signs of 'grief'. It could be dramatised just once, not oftener: the effect would be to make the text tighter, stronger.

I admit that now and then, in tired moments when I sat back and became aware of how my neck ached and how the heat was solidifying and pressing on me, I did wonder if what I was doing was my brief – to render a faithful translation of Suvarna Devi's work. But then I would get up, fetch myself a glass of water from the big clay jar that rested on the ledge of the kitchen window and kept the water marginally cooler than what emerged from the tap, return to my table and take a sip. Then ideas would come to me like drops of moisture falling on the arid manuscript, reviving my interest.

Picking up my pen, I would remind myself that the best

translations are the most inspired, when the translator becomes fully a co-author of the work so that it is a coming together of two creative spirits in a single venture. If the translator cannot rise to that, then the translation will be a failure.

It made me laugh, almost, to see how improved the text was with the changes I had made, and the paring away of repetition. Oh, I should have been an editor – Tara should have employed me in her publishing house – and Suvarna Devi ought to have had an editor before she had a translator. Now she had both. How could she be anything but pleased? My translation was an uncovering, a revealing of what had been buried, concealed in her work. In a way, you could say I was the writer, only I would not be given the recognition. Not by Tara who had not read the original, and not by Suvarna Devi who was unlikely to read the translation. She had said, in the speech she gave at the conference, that although she could read English, she could not write in it because its vocabulary did not 'cover' – that was her word – *her* experience of life. I had thought that a strange remark but now I found reassurance in it. It had been my role to prove that it *could*. Perhaps one day we would meet again and I would explain to her the different way of translation I had discovered: a transcreation? or even a collaboration?

All this was clear to me in the day, while I worked, but I have to confess that darkness, sleeplessness and anxiety made the nights a different matter. Lying on my back, trying to ignore the heat, the sounds and lights of passing traffic, I found that the thoughts and worries I could hold at bay in daylight approached me like ghosts, like monsters come to threaten me. They exerted a weight on my chest and sometimes I could hardly breathe. I would have to get up to try and escape them. I would go to the kitchen and pour myself a glass of water. I would drink it standing by the window and looking out on the deserted street. The street lights would be shining. Sometimes a dog appeared to scavenge in a pile of garbage left outside a tea stall, now shuttered. Occasionally an empty bus passed by, probably returning, at this hour, to the depot. I tried to distract myself with these sights of the ordinary world, but in my mind it was the lines I had been translating and the lines that I had been writing that remained in the forefront. I longed for sleep to obliterate them but it eluded me. Perhaps everything would be normal again once I had sent off the manuscript, I thought, and looked forward to completing the work.

In the interval between handing over the manuscript to Tara and the appearance of the published book, Prema returned to teaching, much to her students' regret. They found her more harsh and ill-tempered than ever and were certain that if she had had a love affair, it must have come to a bitter end. In the staff room, Prema's colleagues asked her how her work had gone during her leave of absence; she answered curtly and seemed unwilling to speak of it. The college librarian asked her to be sure to give her a copy when it was published, and Prema only nodded.

When Tara telephoned to let her know the advance copies had arrived, she did go across to collect them, and Tara found her oddly subdued. Not elated as she might have been at the sight of the beautiful little volume with its cover of pale ochre like the clay of a village wall, a painted window frame in the centre for illustration, arresting in its simplicity.

'Don't you like it?' Tara asked, looking curiously at Prema's grey and drawn face. The arduous labour of translating it through the summer had aged and fatigued her, Tara thought.

'I do, I do,' Prema roused herself to say but, curiously, did not open a copy to look inside. Instead she asked, 'Have copies been sent to Suvarna Devi? And the critics?'

'Of course,' Tara assured her. 'Of course. Now we have just to wait to see what they say.'

Prema carried her copy home, laid it on the table, made herself tea, then sat down to open it finally. She could not help feeling moved by the sight of her name in it, under Suvarna Devi's. Then, with increasing tension, she let her eyes drift over the sentences, from one to the other. Together they had made this book, its text, its lilt and rhythm, its images and metaphors. Would Suvarna Devi approve? Then she came across a phrase she knew had not been there in the original, and the gaps where she had deleted what had seemed to her unnecessary repetitions: the death of the grandfather, the weeping and wailing. Would Suvarna Devi notice? If she did, what would she think? Would she acknowledge the improvement Prema had brought about, or would she oppose it? And the critics, would anyone notice? Would she hear from them?

What she could hear was the raucous cawing of the crows outside, balancing on the telephone wires, and they sounded to her more mocking and scolding than ever.

Then there was a long and difficult silence. Reviews of translations were always scant, Tara reminded her. It was this new breed of authors writing in the colonial tongue, English, who hogged all the attention, not only in England but even here in India, disgracefully. The one review that appeared, in a little read but serious political journal, commended Tara's noble venture in commissioning translations and calling attention to so far 'unknown' writing (as though there were no readers of regional languages). The critic called Suvarna Devi's novel an 'important' one but made no reference to the translation.

'We'll have to wait till the regional press reviews come in,' Tara said and, seeing how anxious Prema looked when she came in to enquire, added kindly, 'I'm sure they will be good. It *is* a good translation after all.'

It was not Tara's way to be effusive and she did sound sincere. In fact, she was. So it was a shock when, a few days later, a letter arrived at her office from someone who informed Tara he was Suvarna Devi's nephew. He came at once to the point, which was that he had read the original text written by his aunt and bought a copy of the translation. On reading it, he had found innumerable discrepancies between the two. He went on to list them.

Frowning heavily, Tara wondered if he was pointing out

serious flaws or if he was just nit-picking the way some readers were sure to do, more to prove their superior knowledge than for any other reason. But, she had to conclude on rereading the list several times, he appeared to have reason for complaint. According to him several pages had been cut out of the translation, the role of some of the characters – e.g. the grandfather – had been abbreviated, and the language itself diverged wildly from the original text. As a native speaker of the language, he felt a responsibility and wished the translator and the publisher to know that he objected strenuously to this 'cavalier attitude' to his aunt's work. He was debating whether to inform her; he did not wish to disturb or upset her, knowing how gentle and sensitive a person she was, but he demanded an explanation for the way she had been treated by Tara's press. What did Tara propose to do? Was she going to continue to bring out these 'spurious' equivalents for the English-speaking elite of what was so much more powerful and beautiful in the original? He advised her against putting out any more of them 'to hoodwink the public'.

Tara put off all meetings for the day and sent for her secretary in order to dictate two letters, one to the nephew to apologise for 'any errors and shortcomings in the translation' and another to the leading newspaper in his aunt's home town to assure them 'appropriate measures were being taken to ensure that in future only rigorously supervised and faithful translations' would be published by her press. cc Prema Joshi.

Eventually Tara's secretary forwarded a packet of letters to

Prema sent by other readers with the same objections – not very many since those who read the original did not necessarily read the translation as well. Also a letter that arrived from Suvarna Devi, written on her yellow stationery with the red rose imprint, thanking her for sending the copies of her book which she said 'looked very nice', and making no mention of the translation. Nor was there any hint of suspicion or attack. Either her nephew had not informed her of his findings or she had chosen to overlook them; she did, after all, have other, possibly more compelling interests in life. Tara did not withdraw the book nor did she ever order a reprint.

The Association of Indian Publishers sent Prema, c/o Tara, an invitation to its next gathering of authors and translators. Prema declined, pleading illness.

So I haven't given up teaching. I continue to go through the same texts with my students. I know they are bored by me. I know they make fun of me behind my back. And I know the principal is waiting for me to retire so she can bring in someone new, someone who will arouse enthusiasm among the students. But, if I do that, what would I do with the rest of my life? That stretches out before me like an empty, unlit road.

Sometimes, on the bus going home from work, I look at the others seated beside me and across from me. Or, rather, since I don't like staring at people's faces, I look down at their feet, shod in slippers or sandals or dusty shoes of cracked leather, and the packages they are holding on their knees, and I think:

that is how I must look to them – a tired woman going home from work with nothing to look forward to, nothing to smile about. Whyever did I imagine I was different, and could live differently from them? We are all in this together, this world of loss and defeat. All of us, every one of us, has had a moment when a window opened, when we caught a glimpse of the open, sunlit world beyond, but all of us, on this bus, have had that window close and remain closed.

It is not that I did not try to open that window again. I gave up, of course, the idea of translating another book, though it meant giving up the language I had acquired with such ardour. In the course of those sleepless nights I spent, a thought did come to me – that I might write a book of my own. It would be an original work, it would draw from no one else and no one else's work. I did feel I owed Suvarna Devi a debt for teaching me, but now it was for me to prove I could establish my own worth as a writer.

For a while I felt excited by that idea – as if the window had opened again, a little, and some light was slanting through it. I had had an idea that bifurcated into more ideas, and I followed these paths with a stirring of hope and delight. The one that drew me more powerfully than any other was the story of my parents' marriage. Their short-lived marriage and its sad end. By writing their stories, I could bring in all the different aspects of my life – the ones I inherited from my mother, her language and her background, and the ones I inherited from my father. I felt the story had promise and even sat down with a large new notebook I purchased from the store across the street, propped my feet up and started scribbling, trying out these themes.

I worked hard at it but whatever pleasure or hope I had had at the outset dissipated. There were scenes I could write in English but other scenes called out to be written in my mother's language. I was torn between the two and could settle on neither. I wrote scraps in one, then scraps in the other, but tore them all up and threw them away: who would read such a jumble?

I was sitting in the dark one evening, listening to the crows on the telephone lines and the lopped tree outside as they quarrelled over their roosting places for the night, hoarse with combat, when it occurred to me that only Suvarna Devi could write this story. Only she had the voice for it; I did not. I had been writing under her influence, with her voice; it was not mine. In adopting hers, I had lost mine.

Then, browsing through a bookshop as I often did on a Saturday morning, I looked up from a display of discounted books spread out on a table and saw a young man I recognised at once as Suvarna Devi's nephew. He had his little son with him, now a toddler, and was pointing out to him some colourful children's books.

For a second I felt panic and wondered if I could slip away unseen. But then I decided that would be cowardly, and I went round the table to face him.

I wondered if he would recognise me but it was clear that he did. I greeted him and asked after his wife and daughter, and then his aunt. He seemed perfectly pleased to see me again and told me they were all well. After that I hesitated, not sure whether to refer to her books, her writing. Perhaps he hesitated too, slightly, but then, smiling, informed me that not only was she well but 'working as hard as ever. Now she has started a school – a primary school for tribal children. She was always so interested in their education. She is working full-time with them and asked me to select some books to send them.' He beamed with pride, then became distracted by his son who had grabbed at some books and was pulling them off a shelf with delight.

So I said goodbye, asking him to convey my regards to his aunt, and in the hubbub of the shopkeeper coming to reprimand the child and the young father's flustered apologies, I left.

The Artist of Disappearance

NOBODY CLIMBED THAT hill any more. Not unless they wished to retreat. It was a good place for that: a retreat. Just the burnt-out remains of the house that had stood there. Only a few walls still standing, a makeshift roof of zinc sheets in place of the turrets and towers that had been there, the rest just blackened stones, ashes, rubble, charred beams, weeds crowding into gaping windows. An occasional newt slipping silently by.

But Ravi was there, sitting on the stone steps that led up to the veranda. It was what he had always done in the evenings when he returned to the house, to listen for the sound of a cowbell ringing faintly and intermittently downhill, then more clearly and metallically as the beast drew closer. Mingled with that tolling was the noise of goat hooves clicking smartly on the stony path, and the goats' small eager bleats as they anticipated the food that would be waiting for them. They were the first to arrive at the homestead below, hunger quickening their pace and dancing approach. Then the cow, eager too but with more body to trundle along a path too narrow for her bony breadth. She had to be encouraged by the flick of a switch that her owner wielded with one hand while with the other he steadied on top of his head the bundle of firewood he had gathered.

And when these shapes appeared in the clearing below, the dogs that had been slumbering the afternoon away scrambled to their feet with an air of importance to show they were alert to their duties, and let out sharp yelps of welcome to announce their arrival to the family that lived there.

The children began to chase the chickens into their pen for the night. The mother called for firewood to be brought in. Smoke unwound in a spool from the gaps in the thatch of the roof. The goats were directed into an enclosure, walled with thorns, by showing them a tin basin in which bits of broken bread had been soaked in warm water, and the cow was led into her shed, with its comfortable smells of dung and straw, to be milked.

Then there was a lull as the activity shifted indoors where a fire of sticks crackled, a pot boiled and the aroma of food was conjured. Around it the children gathered on their haunches, tin plates before them, waiting. The father lowered himself onto a stool, and the mother was finally ready to ladle out the meal she had prepared.

But the older of the two boys remained standing by the door, knowing his role in the day's duties. He took the enamel dish from his mother's hands: she had filled it with rice and dhal into which she threw a handful of green chillies. She gave

him a tin lid to cover the plate and by a slight shift of her chin
– which bore a small blue tattoo – she indicated he was to take
it, take it up.

The boy nodded, then set off up the hill: he knew he should
be quick so as not to let the food cool and congeal. Besides,
he was eager to return for his share. So he climbed the hill as
quickly as he could without tripping or spilling.

When the boy appeared with the covered dish, instead of
merely nodding to indicate he should put it down, Ravi startled him by speaking instead. His voice was hoarse, he used it
so seldom, and it was clear it cost him great effort to speak.

His voice rasping, he asked, 'Have they gone?'

The boy nodded, yes.

'You are sure?'

Yes, the boy nodded again.

Then Ravi took the dish from him, and even mumbled
thanks, adding, 'Tell your father I will not be coming down
tonight.'

Yes, the boy nodded, he would. Duty done, he turned and
went flying downhill to his own meal, and gave three sharp
whistles as he leapt from one stone to the next, to mark his
freedom. The dogs came running up to meet him with their
own eager, hungry barks.

Up at the burnt house, Ravi finished his meal and set the
plate down on the step beside him, then took a biri out of his
shirt pocket, lit it and leaned back against one of the veranda
posts which was still standing, and waited for the sounds of

the household below to subside into silence and the light to withdraw from the valley and climb the hills till only their peaks were lit by the sun. Then they too faded into dusk but he continued to sit there, listening for the last calls of a lone cuckoo to die out and the rustle of the flying squirrel that lived under the eaves as it crept out and launched itself into the evening air where the bats were now swooping and plunging after insects.

He stubbed out the biri, then drew a matchbox out of his shirt pocket and began to play with it, thoughtfully; he might have been a monk with his prayer beads. When he looked up from it he found the woolly dusk had knitted him into the evening scene, inextricably. Silence had fallen on the homestead below and the light of its small fire had sunk and gone out.

He got to his feet and made his way to the bushes encroaching on the house. He lowered his trousers and there was a sound of urine trickling on the stones at his feet. Then he turned and retraced his steps. Picking up the empty dish, he carried it across the veranda to the one area that might still be called a room: it had walls, it was covered, and it held the string cot that Bhola had fetched for him from the hut below, and the few remnants salvaged from the fire, lined up against the blackened wall. Ravi fumbled his way to a table, scarred by the knives and choppers of its kitchen past, on which a kerosene lantern stood. He lit it – there, another match gone – and surveyed the sorry items: an overstuffed chair on which he never sat, a hatstand which held neither a hat nor a walking stick – and saw they were all still there, mute and untouched, as if waiting for the day when they would be chopped up for firewood.

All else that the house had once contained – and there had been an abundance – was gone, just like the leather suitcases that used to be lined up in the hall – the hall! – waiting to be carried out, past the grandfather clock and the portraits of his ancestors, tinted photographs that leaned away from the wall to look down as his father unhooked his favourite walking stick from the hatstand and the astrakhan cap that he liked to wear when travelling, then gave the soft, polite whistle with which he might summon his wife who was detained in her dressing room – her dressing room! – by some last-minute adjustment to her toilet.

While they waited for her to emerge, the father turned to look at the boy standing half hidden by the door to his room, one leg locked around the other, and gave him a playful wink as he set the astrakhan cap jauntily on his head. 'Like it? I bought it in Berlin, I'll have you know, on the Kurfürsten-damm. Can you say that – "Kur-fürst-en-damm"? It had started to snow and I went into this very elegant shop and a most polite gentleman came out from the back to see what I wanted. I pointed it out to him and when I walked out, I had it on my head – just so!' and he gave another wink. 'I'll let you wear it one day – when you can say "Kur-fürst-en-damm",' he offered, and the child knew it was an offer that would evaporate along with all the others and looked away in embarrassment at how glibly his father lied.

99

Then his mother emerged, smelling powerfully of flowers – rose and lily of the valley – dressed in a sage-green sari with a narrow trim of embroidery. 'We must hurry or we'll miss the train,' she cried as if it were the others who had kept her waiting.

Hari Singh, who was waiting at the foot of the stairs, came up to lift one suitcase onto his head and grasp two others in his hands, then carried these out to the waiting automobile that would take them to the railhead in Dehra Dun. The chauffeur came up to carry down the rest.

At the foot of the stairs the parents remembered to turn round and wave at the boy. 'We're off now!' the father announced. 'Be good!' he added, and the mother called out, 'We'll bring you back –' but forgot what she had promised to bring back and left it up in the air. This didn't matter because whatever expensive or elaborate toy it was, it would only be locked up for safe keeping once unpacked and briefly revealed for his tentative admiration.

He sidled down the stairs to the front door and watched the car proceed slowly down the gravelled drive, then disappear under the oak trees that closed behind it like dark stage curtains. For a while he could hear the engine grinding uphill to the motor road, then gave up trying to follow its progress. If it had been night he would have been able to see the lights as they slowly descended downhill to the valley, but it was still afternoon.

And then he could let out the breath he had been holding inside his chest till it swelled into a balloon, tight against his

ribs. A balloon he held pinched between his thumb and fore-
finger and could now set free. Off it went with a whistle, twisting
and turning and wriggling, till it descended, hollowed, into the
limp rubber norm of normality.

Not only he but everyone, everything experienced that
moment. Hari Singh, recovering, took his cloth cap off his head
and was suddenly upright, divested of the posture and demeanour
of servanthood. Coming back up the stairs to the veranda, he
shouted, 'Come on, come on! Let us go and hunt tigers, you
and I!'

Not that they would – Hari Singh was no more given to
keeping his promises than were the boy's parents, but just to
hear the invitation made, loudly and heartily, changed the air,
the atmosphere, and Hari's son Bhola, who had been waiting
behind the bushes, catapult in hand, appeared to see if Ravi
would now come out to play.

Outdoors was freedom. Outdoors was the life to which he
chose to belong – the life of the crickets springing out of the
grass, the birds wheeling hundreds of feet below in the valley
or soaring upwards above the mountains, and the animals invisible in the undergrowth, giving themselves away by an occasional rustle or eruption of cries or flurried calls; plants following
their own green compulsions and purposes, almost impercep-
tibly, and the rocks and stones, seemingly inert but mysteri-
ously part of the constant change and movement of the earth.
One had only to be silent, aware, observe and perceive – and
this was Ravi's one talent as far as anyone could see.

Outdoors, Ravi had watched as a snake shed itself of its old skin, emerging into a slithering new length, leaving behind on the path a shroud, transparent as gauze, fragile as glass. Once he had come upon a tree with long, cream-coloured cylinders for flowers, attracting armies of ants coming to raid their fabled sweetness and sap, armies that would not be deflected by the intervention of a stick, a twig, and would persist till they reached the treasure, and drowned.

Outdoors, the spiders spun their webs in tall grass, a spinning you would not observe unless you became soundless, motionless, almost breathless and invisible, as when he had seen a praying mantis on a leaf exactly the same shade of green as itself, holding in its careful claws a round, striped bee buzzing even as it was devoured, which halted when its eyes swivelled towards him and became aware it was being watched.

And there was always the unexpected – lifting a flat stone and finding underneath an unsuspected scorpion immediately aroused and prepared for attack, or coming across an eruption from the tobacco-dark leaf mould of a family of mushrooms with their ghostly pallor and caps, hats and bonnets, like refugees that had arrived in the night.

Or a troop of silver-haired, black-masked monkeys bounding through the trees to arrive with war whoops, or sporting like trapeze artists at a circus, then disappearing like actors from a stage that the forest provided.

And everywhere were the stones – flat blue splinters of slate, pebbles worn to an irresistible silkiness by the weather and that could be collected and arranged according to size and colour in an infinite number of patterns and designs, none of which were ever repeated or fixed.

Infinite – unless you were like Bhola who always brought with him a catapult and almost automatically raised it whenever he saw a dove or a squirrel that could be brought down with a shot. Ravi was not for such sport; a heap of dead feathers or fur were for him as unnatural as for the slain creature. Ravi was interested only in the variations and mutations of the living, their innumerable possibilities.

It was as if the curtains came down on all this, if not entirely obliterated it, when the monsoon rose up in thunderous clouds from the parched valley below to engulf the hills, invade them with an opaque mist in which a pine tree or a mountain top appeared only intermittently, and then unleashed a downpour that brought Ravi's rambling to a halt and confined him to the house for days at a time, deafened by the rain drumming on the rooftop and cascading down the gutters and through the spouts to rush downhill in torrents.

Everything in the house turned damp; the blue fur of mildew crept furtively over any object left standing for the briefest length of time: shoes, bags, boxes, it consumed them all. The sheets on the bed were clammy when he got between them at night, and the darkness rang with the strident cacophony of the big tree crickets that had been waiting for this, their season. From the pond down in the clearing below came the gleeful bellowing of bullfrogs. Lying awake, listening, Ravi wished he could slip out with Hari Singh's big flashlight and catch them in its beam, but perhaps the gleam emitted by the fireflies flitting among the trees by the thousands would be light enough. He shivered with cold and anticipation.

But Hari Singh locked him in carefully every night, and by day filled his ears with tales of the leopards that came out of the forest to prey on any poor goat or calf left outdoors and were known to carry away even the fierce bhutia dogs people kept to guard their homes and livestock. What chance had a small, thin boy like Ravi against such creatures? Hari Singh demanded as he served Ravi his dinner at one end of the dining table, standing by with a dishcloth over his shoulder. While Ravi picked at his food, Hari Singh talked of his glory days when Ravi's grandfather had taken him on hunting expeditions and allowed him to carry the guns with which he shot the bears, deer and panthers whose pelts, horns and glass-eyed heads watched Ravi make his way through his meal. Of course the boy ate very little, his mouth hanging open with wonder as he listened, and consequently Hari Singh gave up setting a place at the table with the requisite glass and silverware, and took to letting Ravi eat his meals at a small table out on the veranda where he would not be separated from the outdoor world that provided all the nourishment he wanted. When it rained he gave Ravi his food on a plate and set him on a stool in a corner of the kitchen by the sooty glow of the kitchen fire while he himself smoked a biri which he was strictly forbidden to do when the parents were present.

The only visitor to the house during the long summers when the parents were away was the teacher they had employed to supervise Ravi's homework, a Mr Benjamin who taught at one of the many boarding schools strung out along the ridge, and supplemented his income by giving private tuition on the side. The parents approved of him because he always wore a suit and tie and spoke in what approximated to 'good English', so they did not look too far into his qualifications for teaching their son mathematics whose strong subject it was not (nor was it Mr Benjamin's). Ravi wished the subject might be something else – ornithology, for instance, or geology, but Mr Benjamin regarded himself as far above such frivolous matters. He cleared his throat on arriving, hung up his walking stick and umbrella, scraped his shoes ferociously on the doormat to dislodge the dirt they had collected on the way to the house on the hilltop, wondering aloud what had possessed Ravi's parents to live so far from the civilised centre of Mussoorie (though he knew perfectly well that Ravi's father had inherited the house from *his* father who had owned a brewery in these parts and used to come up from Bombay ostensibly to inspect the brewery but actually for the shikar and its trophies). Then Mr Benjamin would tell Ravi to open his books and get to work.

As the afternoon dragged sluggishly on, Ravi drooped lower and lower over the smudged and spotted copybook, chewing at his pencil till it splintered and had to be spat out, for which he received a smart whack on the head from Mr Benjamin's ruler. He could hear Hari Singh's children playing in the clearing below, their rooster crowing, their goats bleating, and he grew despondently aware of the afternoon light dying all the while.

But Mr Benjamin stayed till punctually at four o'clock Hari Singh brought him a cup of hot tea frothing with milk and thick with sugar. Ah-h, the tutor sighed, and let slip his professional manner enough to pour out a bit from the cup into the saucer and blow on it, then slurp it up blissfully. Ah-h, ah-h. It was not what he would do in front of his employers but of course Ravi was not that and all Ravi was thinking was that Hari Singh needed somehow to be persuaded to bring in the tea earlier. When Mr Benjamin came reluctantly to the end of this sweet pleasure, he gave Ravi a few more taps of the ruler to remind him he was only a miserable schoolboy and ought to be attending to his schoolwork instead of staring at him open-mouthed, then picked up his walking stick and umbrella and disappeared into the floating mists of the monsoon.

Why did his parents never take him with them when they travelled abroad? The boy never asked and they never explained. It seemed they believed the child belonged at home while they belonged to the wider world where of course they would not have the time for him (or a servant to see to his needs). One day, they said, he would be old enough to accompany them and it occurred to no one that there was no reason he could not accompany them now. (What was not said, never even mentioned, was that they were a childless couple, Ravi the child they had adopted – at the suggestion of a distant, philanthropic aunt – yet as far as anyone could see, they never made up a family.) And of course, in a way, their absence *was* his vacation, which came to an end when the parents returned.

Their return coincided with the beginning of the school year – the taking out and putting on of grey flannels and crimson blazer with a crest on the pocket proclaiming a Latin aspiration no one understood, the knotting of a noose-like tie under the shirt collar; each day a slower and more reluctant walk uphill to the prison of the school buildings grouped around a courtyard from which rose a roar that bubbled fiercely as a kettle on the boil till a gong was struck and the kettle was abruptly lifted off the fire. Rows of boys filed off to the regime of lessons administered by furious teachers who threw chalk at one or twisted another's ear, picking on the most miserable targets to punish in inventive and fiendish ways. This was considered the only way in which the Latin motto that no one understood might be upheld.

After that treatment – and Ravi was too ashamed to tell anyone or even admit to himself that he was the inquisitors' favourite target – he could not turn light-heartedly to the escapades of his fellow victims who lingered around the school gates after classes to watch the girls in their pleated skirts and green sweaters come out of the adjoining school, and attempt to lure them, sometimes, sometimes successfully, with the promise of an ice cream at Magnolia's or a film show at the Picture Palace. Ravi was too crushed by the school day to take the risk of any other failure, and heaved his school bag onto his back to slink home with the hope of going unnoticed – which he mostly was.

To be released from school meant only being released into the house where the parents now presided. If they did not use a ruler to crack across his head, or throw things at him in a rage, they had other ways to plunge their son into misery. The house, in their presence, had a set of rigid rules. The bell rang at intervals, punctually (punctuality being one cardinal mark of their Westernised ways), table manners had to be observed meticulously (another of those cardinal marks of which they possessed an arsenal), each infraction was pounced on and corrected (spare the rod etc. was the maxim by which they had been raised so they thought of themselves as permissive), and great lengths of time went by at the table as soup was followed by an entrée which was followed by a pudding which was followed by a savoury, some with enticing names – 'angels on horseback'! – which they never lived up to.

And then there was the entertaining they did which required his complete invisibility and silence while the parents played bridge and canasta and drank tea or cocktails. There was a certain pleasure to be had in hiding in the kitchen and watching Hari Singh arrange a tea tray or whip egg whites for a pudding and being slipped a sweet or a savoury titbit – but there were also the hours he had to sit more or less confined to a chair, swinging his legs till his own supper and bedtime could be seen to, also by Hari Singh.

It was better when his parents dressed up, sprayed themselves with exotic Parisian perfumes, got into their car and went out – but this did not happen nearly often enough for Ravi because his parents went abroad during what was known as 'the season' in Mussoorie, when British society came up to the hills to 'escape' from 'the plains' and brought their plays, balls, charades and garden parties with them.

Ravi's father sometimes said, wistfully, 'Why don't we spend the summer here for once, Tehmi? It's very jolly, I'm told,' but Tehmi had been brought up – in Bombay and at finishing school in Switzerland – to think summers had to be spent in Nice or Montreux where many of her family were now ensconced. Sometimes the father went on to complain, 'It's a damned expense, you know, Tehmi,' which made her screw her face into an expression of distaste at the mention of anything so unmentionable.

Fortunately for him, the father, these excursions were brought to an end when war broke out. Although the family liquor business flourished as never before, it was out of the question to risk a sea voyage when ships were being regularly torpedoed. And Mussoorie had never been as gay as now, nor its salubrious climate so needed for the health and recreation of the British soldiers on leave from the war fronts in Burma, Malaya and Singapore, and it was incumbent on the ladies of Mussoorie to provide them with the fun and relaxation that was their due.

The father was finally able to enjoy their exile in Mussoorie in what had been his father's 'hunting lodge' (once his brothers and uncles had discovered the disasters he could create in their business and the need to keep him away). He could now go to dances at Hackman's every night he liked, in his evening clothes with a silk scarf thrown over his shoulders and the astrakhan cap he had purchased in Berlin set rakishly on his head gleaming with pomade. He literally danced his way through one pair of shiny patent leather shoes after another. He would come home with a breath as fierce as a dragon's and putrid as a tiger's, singing his way to bed, and Ravi in the room next door cowered under his blankets to shut out the horror of it.

It was his mother who wilted in these years. She went with her husband to the parties and dances but it was clearly not her milieu and not her style. She set out, as exquisitely dressed as always, but drawing her light summer shawl about her as if she needed its protection, and with an expression on her face not radiant or expectant but rather as if she was about to swallow an unpleasant potion. She would not dance with the English officers and watched from among a group of likewise scandalised but dutiful wives, as her Hosni went blithely up to the English WAAFs and invited them to dance. Most of them were amused by this little man who did not seem to understand his place, and many accepted: he was an excellent dancer if a bit of a show-off.

And he had the comeuppance anyone might have predicted: a British army officer recently up from the battlefields and probably more deeply affected by what he had experienced than anyone knew, and royally drunk, objected to this little dark man dancing like an organ-grinder's monkey with his wife, and followed him out to where his car was waiting. In another age he might have challenged him to a duel but these were more brazen times and he simply lifted his baton and let the upstart have it on the head, the shoulders, the back, till Hosni's chauffeur was able to get him away, bundle him into their car and escape.

Ravi's mother did not return to what was known as Mussoorie society. The father, on recovering, lifted up his chin – sticking-plastered – and insisted on going out in a show of pride that might be considered nationalistic or merely pig-headed, but he did not go to Hackman's again, nor did he attempt to re-enter British society. He kept to the more familiar Indian scene – bridge games, sedate celebrations of anniversaries of one kind or another, and many hours in the club bar. His wife kept mostly to her room and even to her bed. It was not she who had been injured – not physically – but anyone who cared to analyse her condition would have said 'her spirit' had suffered a blow. All they actually said was that poor Tehmi's asthma had taken a turn for the worse.

Ravi was seldom invited into his mother's bedroom; her nerves would not stand it. But at this time a fourth person was admitted into their household and, like a fourth wheel attached to a wobbling carriage, provided some balance to what had become so seriously unbalanced.

No one would have thought Miss Dora Wilkinson capable

of such a feat of engineering. She had been recruited from a home for indigent British ladies although she had few skills to show for herself. She was undeniably elderly and her once blonde hair and once blue eyes had faded to grey. Hosni turned away from interviewing her as a possible companion to his wife with a look of unconcealed disappointment, but for that very reason she was thought eminently suitable for the position: she would certainly not ask for leave to go to an afternoon dance. She could not even join her employers for a game of whist. But she did her best to provide a bit of nursing in the form of a dab of 4711 cologne or a cup of tea, and she could read aloud in a somewhat tremulous voice the sonnets of Elizabeth Barrett Browning and of Christina Rossetti. Her presence was immensely soothing to the mother for this and also for another reason, unspoken and perhaps unconscious: the woman's pale skin and light eyes and English diction made up in some inexplicable way for the treatment that her husband had suffered, the humiliation of it. Here was Miss Wilkinson bathing her brow with eau de cologne and helping her sip consommé from a cup of delicate china, and it was good to know, soothing to know, that such things could also be.

Her only fault, apart from her age, was that she had a cat. The cat was forbidden anywhere near the asthmatic's bedroom and expected to be kept confined to Miss Wilkinson's quarters. Ravi would shyly ask if he could enter in order to study the cat, his first experience of an animal as 'a pet'. He was not sure if he liked a 'pet' animal or if it merely seemed a curiosity, unrelated to the wild world where she belonged, but he liked to sit on a stool, his chin cupped in his hands, and gaze at her. She too seemed unsure if she approved of him and, folding her two front paws under her chin and narrowing her green eyes into slits to observe him discreetly, gave no hint that she was doing so other than to start if he made the slightest move. They were held by mutual fascination, nervous apprehension and an irresistible attraction.

Only Miss Wilkinson smiled and smiled, certain there had never been so harmonious a society. This earned Ravi her undying gratitude. She would ask him to do little favours for her (really for the awkward adolescent's sake as much as for hers), find her a feather for a bookmark or bring her some flowers for her vase. He would flush with pride at being asked and stumble off to pull some passion-fruit flowers off a vine over the veranda balustrade or pick out a blue magpie's tail feather he had found on the hillside, a prized possession of his. She received them with extravagant praise and thanks.

The father, almost as if he realised he had no further role to play, allowed the car to carry him, after an evening of bridge at the club, into the pouring rain that had washed away large tracts of the sharply curving road and down a landslide that had not shown in the beam of the headlights in the driving rain, halfway into the khud where it crashed into a pine tree with such force that the vehicle was almost split in two. The villagers who found him and the driver, and carried them to the hospital on the ridge, sent a message to the family that he was not seriously injured and would recover (about the driver they could make no such sanguine prognosis for he was already dead), but they proved wrong: he died that night of internal injuries just after asking for a brandy but before he could consume it.

The years that followed, Ravi did not count. He did not count them because he did not acknowledge them as his: they did not belong to his life because they did not belong to the forest and the hills. They belonged to the family in Bombay, to the business office, to his duties there, his relations to the family, and some years at a college studying 'management' (although they never made clear and he never understood what he was supposed to 'manage'). One might think these would yield a full volume of incident and event, but it was as if Ravi, encased in a block of grey cement, could see nothing, hear nothing and say nothing either.

He knew the family thought him freakishly backward, a wild creature from the mountains. His cousins sometimes sniggered as he passed them. An aunt would raise her finger to her head and wriggle it like a loose screw when she thought he was not looking.

Once they picnicked by the sea. It was the only time he recalled seeing the Indian Ocean. Of course this could not be true since Bombay is an island city and the sea lies all around it, but he had never been taken closer to it than in a passing automobile. On this occasion he actually broke free to clamber across some rocks exposed by the receding tide and gulped down lungfuls of soggy sea air as if he were gulping lungfuls of life-saving oxygen. Everywhere were pools left scattered among the streaming wet rocks, and he walked into them blindly, socks and shoes still on, dazed by this glittering aquatic world he had not known existed. He went down on his knees in the wet sand and stared into one such pool, his face dropping lower and lower, very nearly into it. He felt it could take an entire life to study the strange, extraordinary life that teemed in it – minute, multifarious and totally unlike any earthbound equivalent. But the family sent the servant boy they had brought along to facilitate the picnic to seize him by his sleeve, haul him to his feet and lead him back to where they sat, scandalised, on a mat spread out of range of the sea.

He might have been their prisoner and, like any prisoner, was despised and mistreated to the precise degree that mistreatment could go without detection. The room he was given had formerly been a storeroom and was still blocked by broken furniture and packed boxes. Its one window opened onto the garbage chute of the building. Neighbours tossed bags of refuse into the chute out of their kitchen and bathroom windows; its walls were streaked black, yellow and green and the odour rose to his window in thick coils. He became convinced he would die here and then be placed in a garbage bag and dropped into the miasma himself. There was no one to whom he could explain that in order to survive he needed to be at altitude, a Himalayan altitude, so he might breathe.

He might very well have suffocated if he had stayed longer. As it was he really did not know how long it was – months? years? – before news came that his mother had been moved into intensive care at the hospital, followed by news of her death. Thus, release – hers followed by his.

Perhaps he babbled and laughed like a madman on the journey back, perhaps not. But he remembered leaping onto the platform before the train had quite come to a halt at the station in Dehra Dun, nearly falling onto his knees, then fighting his way onto a bus to Mussoorie (his relatives in Bombay would not have believed his ferocity). For a while he continued, desperate: it did not look as if the bus could free itself of the city traffic, and then the country traffic – the other buses and huge, lumbering trucks loaded with rocks, logs, sacks and bundles and men perched on top, their mouths and noses wrapped in scarves against the dust and fumes of exhaust. Where was the silence that he remembered, or the solitude? he asked himself in a frenzy of impatience, till he realised that each turn in the twisting road was carrying him higher and higher and the air that blew in through the open windows was cooler, fresher, drier, air he could draw into his lungs in long draughts because it blew, he believed, from the snows themselves, half imagined, half perceived, a pale scribble against a pale sky.

Here the forest began. Here a monkey clan sat on a strip of wall, grooming each other and watching the passing buses for a handful of peanuts or a banana tossed out by the laughing passengers. Here a rivulet tumbled over rocks and a rough shelter built of stones and sticks straddled it. Here a pine tree leaned precariously over a cliff, its trunk split in two by lightning. Here an orange grove grew in a green clearing, its fruit glowing bright. The dust and odour of the city and plains left behind, the bus rose higher into the mountains where these were replaced by the sharp sweetness of pine woods, the smoke of wood fires, the glass-like clarity of mountain air.

He covered the last stretch on foot, rediscovering the paths that led out of the town, downhill into the forest, and through it to where the house stood, its roof showing above the tree-tops. Birds sent out their long, fluting calls in spirals that he returned to them in long, fluting whistles through the silence.

Silence, but not solitude: Miss Wilkinson remained. It seemed cruel to send her back, after his mother's death, to the home for indigent British ladies which was by then close to collapse, with no funds now that the British were gone to repair or staff it, so that whoever still lived there and had not been sent or fetched away, lived in a ruin and increasingly resembled one themselves.

Ravi, finding her in a state of despair at the thought of being made to leave the family of cats she had stealthily acquired over time, assured her she need not, that she could stay and 'run the house' for him – as he thought to tell her in a moment of inspiration. It was clear that Miss Wilkinson could run nothing, not the house nor her own life. She had never confessed to anyone that her eyesight had been deteriorating over the years, the spectacles she wore less than useless, and for years she had been reciting not reading the poems of Christina Rossetti to her employer who did not miss the dropped line or forgotten word. When Ravi returned, he suspected her of being quite blind and only pretending not to be. The manner in which she fumbled and felt her way around the room gave her away and she no longer ventured out of it, though her cats slipped in and out freely, having the run of the place now. Hari Singh had retired and gone to live in his village in Tehri, leaving his son Bhola in charge, and it was Bhola who brought her meals cooked by his wife in the hut below, and provided her with a small paraffin stove on which to make herself tea if she wanted a cup when she could not sleep at night.

Ravi had not thought, after his time in Bombay, that he would ever want to live in proximity with anyone again. He would have revelled in clear space inhabited by no other than a line of ants creeping across the floor by day on their endless forages, the flying squirrel that lodged in the eaves launching itself into space at dusk to go hunting by night, and an occasional snake or scorpion that had lost its way and strayed into his. He was relieved to find that Miss Wilkinson, in her room upstairs next to his parents' empty one, was in no need of anyone either. Her wan aura was tinged by nothing more visible, or audible, than gratitude. She had never learned Hindi and could exchange no words with Bhola when he brought her a bowl of porridge in the morning, her cup of lentil soup at night, but murmured her thanks in English. Only the occasional hiss or growl of one of her cats in combat or competition with another roused her to speak and then she would murmur, 'Oh, Pusskins, is that you again? You naughty you, hmm? And where's old Billy then? You're not fighting poor Billy, are you?' and they would come up and rub themselves against her legs till she herself uttered a kind of low purr of delight.

When Ravi came in at dusk – it was at this time that he had developed the habit of staying outdoors all day, invisibly engaged in an art no one witnessed and he himself barely acknowledged – he would find himself going upstairs to her, surprised that he would seek out anyone's company. Hers was the one presence that did not make him turn and flee. She neither wanted nor asked anything of him. She would hear his step and look up, sightlessly, and the cats would rise to their feet or descend from their perches and come towards him, confident that he would make no loud, sudden movement but simply sink into an armchair beside Miss Wilkinson's where one might reach up to his knees to be stroked or else curl up and go back to sleep. Ravi, on enquiring after Miss Wilkinson's health that day, would reach out to the small row of books on a spindly bamboo stand between them and ask, 'Would you like me to read to you, Miss Wilkinson?'

She nodded but made no suggestion and he would choose something at random. No one else had discovered his talent for reading aloud in a low, modulated voice that scarcely broke the quiet. He found he could not adapt it to the dramatic pauses and the rising and falling tones of poetry which embarrassed him, so he read to her from the books he had brought across from his parents' room, the novels of Trollope and Sir Walter Scott, and she would listen, her head lowered, till she began to nod and her mouth to fall open, her breath coming and going audibly. Sometimes he left her like that, replacing the book and leaving without waking her. Having her in the house was like having a very old pet cat that continued to doze through what was left of its life and did not disturb him beyond an underlying concern over its inevitable end.

No one could have imagined the end she would create for herself, unwittingly or not. Did she merely wake one morning and automatically fumble at the little paraffin stove to make herself tea? Or did she light it to invite an explosion, a conflagration of light in her dark world? Would this harmless, almost ectoplasmic creature choose to light it, then knock it over – she who took such care not to knock into anything – and so set the curtains alight? Was she aware of how one flame split into many within seconds, into an army of advancing swords of fire that charged through the room as if it were made of paper, then poured through the house in an ocean of smoke, sending sparks upwards into the roof beams and downwards along the banisters and stairs?

Probably Ravi became aware of it at almost the same moment she did, opened his door to find the smoke surging towards him, preceded by Miss Wilkinson's crazed, leaping cats, and had to fight against it up the stairs which was already a river of fire.

No one could explain how he made it to Miss Wilkinson's room or, on finding her on her knees attempting to crawl out, lifted her – she might have been a paper doll or a rag in his arms – and brought her down seconds before the stairs cracked and crashed in a great cascade of fire.

Bhola was at the front door, trying to break it down, and the villagers who had been up early and seen the great bonfire billowing up over the oak trees like the millennial sun, were running forward when the two of them emerged, blackened and smouldering themselves. They were caught up and flung down in the dirt to put out the flames, and when the firemen finally arrived they were found seated on the grass, shrouded in ash. The fire had already reached its zenith, and the remains of the house within it a blackened skeleton knee-deep in soot and smoke, contorting and writhing in the heat. Miss Wilkinson was asking for her cats, for Pusskins and Billikins, reaching out her blackened, peeling fingers as if she might encounter them and draw them to her. 'Ravi, Ravi, where are they? Do you see them? Are they here?' 'Don't worry, Miss Wilkinson, don't worry, they'll be back,' he kept saying, for they had either perished in the flames or fled into the forest, he could not know. When an ambulance arrived and he helped to lift her into it, she began to wail, 'I can't go, Ravi, not without them, I can't,' but she did, she had to, and she went, wailing 'Pusskins, Billikins, my dears!' like a ghostly siren. Some of those present were to swear later that it was the cats who were heard wailing.

Ravi knew he could not, although he wished to, leave the

scene himself. He knew he had to wait for the firemen to quench the flames and then enter the ruins with Bhola to see what could be salvaged. By then half the town seemed to have arrived. This was not really so: the house was too far out of town for news to have travelled that fast, but the people from nearby villages up and down the hillside had come running to see the blaze, uncommon at this time of year, just after the rains, although common enough in summer when the forest was dry as tinder and a bolt of lightning could set it on fire. And a fire is always a fine thing to see, a fine thing. So now they milled around, shouting, trying to help and also to catch a glimpse of the recluse who had occupied it. 'Look!' shouted a boy who led a tribe of urchins. 'He's there! I saw him!' 'That's not him, that's Bhola the chowkidar.' 'But look what I found – a spoon. Look, a spoon!' and the firemen had to chase them off to a safe distance from which to watch the undoing of the house.

So Ravi withdrew into the woods and did not return till everyone was gone and Bhola came looking for him with a large flashlight that cut swathes of light through the night forest, startling owls and nightjars. Then he voiced his wish to stay on in the house. He entered the ruin and found the walls of one room still nearly intact as well as its roof. After standing around in disbelief and disapproval for a while, Bhola finally went and fetched him a string cot from his own hut below, and food when he saw Ravi had not given that a thought. He also brought him a kerosene lamp which seemed something of a travesty in that burnt house, and lit it, turning Ravi into a shadow that leapt and clawed at the walls.

He went once to see Miss Wilkinson in the hospital. But she was in the general ward – it was a small one and clean but inevitably there were other patients there and their visitors too. He found he could not sit and he could not speak with all of them watching and listening. The news of the fire had become common knowledge and there was much curiosity, as Ravi ought to have known. All along the road to the hospital people had come out to stand in the doorways and watch him go. He had felt he was being stalked by them and now he was hunted down and trapped.

Aware of his presence in spite of his silence, an unrecognisably shrunken and damaged Miss Wilkinson parted her parched lips to croak, 'You don't need to stay, Ravi. Don't stay.'

He could not bring himself to visit her again. It was agony to him knowing he ought to, that he was the only person who could and should, but he did not.

It cost him an almost unbearable effort to appear when he heard of her death. Instead of following the funeral cortège, which was made up of a priest who had visited the home for indigent ladies (from whose name the word 'British' had long been removed) and a few of the able-bodied still left there, he slipped around the hillside and waited for them at the foot of the British cemetery.

A grave had been dug out at the lower end where it stopped

in a thicket of oak trees and mounds of moss. On the upper slope were tumbled gravestones, mostly covered in lichen, leaving few decipherable words, always the same ones – 'the beloved', 'the devoted' – and here and there a headless angel or a cross in pieces among the ferns. The air at the lower depth was always in the shade and perpetually chill and dank.

Standing to one side, concealed by a tree trunk with low branches – almost as if he were a criminal at the scene of a crime, said those who spied him – he watched the shuffling, mumbling ceremony, before Miss Wilkinson in her plain pine coffin was lowered into the earth. He hoped they had dug the earth deep, that jackals would not come in the night to dig it up, that the heavy rain that fell would not penetrate it, nor the frost in winter. He hoped she had been wrapped in a shawl for warmth, that a pillow had been placed under her head. It seemed the most cruel end to be placed in a pit in the ground and sealed into it so no light reached her and the world of cats and books, tea and touch was shut off. When he heard the earth being shovelled over the coffin, falling on it in clods, he fled.

The children in the villages said he had buried the cats the old lady was said to have had, some of them alive. Others claimed the cats had escaped into the forest and turned into bagad-billas whose glowing amber eyes could be encountered in the dark if you were out late. Some said the cats could be heard wailing as they prowled the ruins at night, and some that the house was haunted by the old lady. They said the recluse had the power to turn himself into a ghost in the night, a bhoot, so he could keep company with her ghost and the cats', then turn back into the wild-haired man in rags who would sometimes emerge from the house by day but immediately disappear if encountered, leaving behind a whiff of smoke. He had that power, they observed, to disappear as if by magic.

They tried to get Bhola to tell them some thrillingly blood-curdling stories about what went on in the ruin, but Bhola had grown as taciturn as his employer, and only grunted a refusal. As for the children he had after his marriage to Manju Rani of Tehri, they never heard such tales either; to them Ravi was the harmless man in the burnt house to whom they carried a plateful of food or a can of kerosene for his lamp and who thanked them without looking up.

He was encountered sometimes by a goatherd or men looking for firewood in the forest, an occasional villager with a bundle on his head and a switch in his hand, on a path leading down-hill – never the path uphill to town. The wild raspberry bushes closed in on the path and one came to a great boulder that looked as if it might fall and block the descent completely in the next monsoon; there the path twisted away and continued down through the lantana bushes and blue-flowering ageratum of the lower hillside to a scattering of stone huts with sheaves of corn and pumpkins drying on their roofs and a stream running past that was straddled by a watermill where the great grinding stones could be heard milling the corn and wheat brought to it. Occasionally they saw Ravi on the path, but always above the level of the boulder, and murmured a greeting as they hurried after their goats or steadied the heavy load on their head, receiving only a grunt in reply.

But at that point, by the boulder, he ceased to be on the path. The boulder might have been a hulking black magician that waited for him to appear, then threw its shadow down on him like a cloak, and spirited him away.

The boulder presented a block to others but not to Ravi: he would slip around and let himself through the crease between it and the hillside, and so into the hollow below where only the merest trickle of water made its way from the lip of the cliff above, if the weather was not too dry. Then he had only to part the branches of the chestnut tree that drooped over the opening to the glade, curtain-like, and let them come together again to conceal him. The liquid flow of this path then entered into the hidden pool of the glade that no one else knew existed.

All signs of the outer world vanished: the distant halloos criss-crossing the terraced fields in the valley below, the barking of a dog in the village on the other side of the stream, the grinding of the stones of the watermill. Only a bird sang, with piercing sweetness, till it noted Ravi's appearance, and took off.

He then prowled around like an animal returning to its shelter: some ferns might have unfolded their tight knots of brown fur and transformed themselves into waving green fans; the family of pallid mushrooms of the day before might now be scattered and lie in shreds of fawn suede tinged with mauve. The leaves of the chestnut could be studied for signs of turning and he would watch and wait for the precise shade of dark honey that he wanted before he collected the leaves and filled the clearing he was making around the strange conical stone at the centre of the hollow. And the broken branch he had found on the way and dragged in with him, once dried and bleached to suggest a skeleton, could be added to the design. The berries he picked along the way could be worked into the creases of the rock so it might seem inlaid with strands of gleaming gems or as if it had sprung veins of precious ore.

He considered enlarging the design by bringing enough pebbles, or perhaps some sand from the stream-bed below, to see how they could be arranged to suggest a pool in which the rock formed an island.

Spider-like, Ravi set to work spinning the web of his vision over the hidden glade. And each day it had to be done before night fell.

It was already dark when the visitors drew up at the tea stall on the ridge, tired and hungry and not too good-tempered. Balram lit the Petromax and it roared to life, its blue flame flaring out and hissing like a demon, making them wince at its aggression.

The girl made a face of annoyance and shaded her eyes.

Chand laughed and shrugged as if it could not be helped, and poured out the beer Balram had brought them. 'Ready to eat?' he asked, because he was.

'You think they'll have anything to eat?'

'Ask.'

They called over to Balram who was making a show of wiping the counter. 'D'you serve food?'

Of course he served food. What did these city slickers up from the plains in their too-heavy jackets and too-new boots take him for, him and his establishment and his town? Resentfully he allowed he could give them samosas, bhajias, two-egg omelettes, three- and four-egg omelettes, as much as they wanted, and in double-quick time.

'Any roti?'

'Roti of course, the best you've ever had,' he told them, at once proud and rude.

'We'll have that, lots. And more beer.'

Sitting at a tin-topped table, they juggled their beer mugs, their plates of food, wolfing it all down ravenously in silence. It was the first meal they had had that day, travelling from the city in the dust of the vast plain, the jeep breaking down again and again in the most inconvenient places, far from any habitation, so that the two men had to take turns at trekking out, cursing and complaining, in search of motor workshops and spare parts to get them moving again. They had done the last stretch, winding steeply uphill, as darkness fell.

Had it really been such a good idea, coming up here to shoot a film on environmental degradation in the Himalayas? It had seemed so, but now they found themselves sinking into the familiar sense of defeat at the start of a project, the stage at which they began to doubt if it could be done.

'Wait till tomorrow, we haven't seen anything yet. We've been told about the quarries and the landslides, the tunnelling and the logging. There should be a lot.'

'Where will we find all this, in a holiday resort? We'd better get a guide,' Chand said, and called over to the tea-stall owner, manager, whoever he was. But how were they to explain what they wanted? Soil erosion, cattle grazing, deforestation: could he ever have heard these terms or given a thought to such matters in his world of a chai dukan and its beer and omelettes?

The man came over reluctantly, flinging his dishcloth over his shoulder. 'My name is Balram,' he told them, sensing he might have further dealings with this lot than just providing them with a meal. These people from the plains needed a lot of help when they came up here, especially if they came outside the tourist season. During the season you could count on them moving in a herd; they could be left to themselves, to prome-nade on the Mall, eyeing the flashy women, looking for bars, hotels, the kind of thing they were used to in the cities. But when they came out of season they came for other reasons.

He had seen the jeep they had driven up in, with its Delhi licence plate and a lot of what looked like expensive luggage, stuff they brought in with them, not wanting to let it out of their sight. Then there was this girl, wearing pants, dark glasses, her hair cut short. Balram was not at all sure he approved. Any daughter of his who went around like that would have got a tight slap from him. People came up from the plains, thought they could get away with that here. He had better show them they couldn't fool him. He saw a lot of that around here, knew a lot. He also had a very fine moustache – small, but kept well trimmed. He touched it for reassurance.

The two men had the decency to half rise from their chairs and shake his hand. Now he knew they really needed him, he relaxed. 'What can I do for you?'

'We have come here to do a few days' shooting,' the older man, who had been picking his teeth and still had a toothpick to chew on, began to explain. Seeing Balram's moustache twitch slightly in curiosity – what kind of shoot: boar, deer, panther, partridge? – he went on: 'To make a film.'

'Oh, a fill-um.' Balram was not nearly as impressed as they seemed to think he might be. Mussoorie had seen any number of films made, actors coming up from Bombay, plump and glossy with success, to dance down the Mall and pose against the mountainscape. Crowds would gather around, gape, shout out lewd comments and hoot with laughter, enjoying the tamasha. Traffic would get blocked, police would be called. 'So you are from Bombay, are you?'

'No, no,' Chand, the younger, the quicker, corrected. 'We make documentaries, for television.'

'Television, hunh?' Balram had been meaning to buy a set for his shop, and would have if the electric supply were more dependable. What was the use of a television without that? he'd said to his son who clamoured for one.

'And the documentary we have come to make is about these hills.'

130

Balram gave a snicker of laughter. 'Many directors come for that. Scenery, they all like scenery.'

'No, we're not interested in that. What we have heard is that the scenery is being spoilt, destroyed. Timber companies are cutting down the trees. Limestone quarries and phosphate mines are making the hills unstable. Soil erosion is taking place. Lots of landslides are occurring. That is what we have come to film.'

Balram could not think of anything more dull, and unnecessary. He fingered his moustache in what was clearly scepticism if not derision.

'So we need to go to spots where this is taking place.'

Now that he saw they needed help, Balram decided to be magnanimous. He waved his hand, offering it all to them as if it were nothing to him. 'You can go,' he gave his permission. 'You can see.'

But to them that sounded too vague and uncertain. They could see this was not his idea of a film. It was not scenic and had no commercial potential.

'Can you get us a guide who can take us to such sites?'

'Hmm.' It was a matter for thought and calculation, not to be dismissed in haste. Balram was a man to act judiciously, not rashly. Possibilities arose. He nodded. 'I will see.'

'But soon?' Chand, anyone could see, was a man in a hurry. Nothing could happen fast enough. When nothing happened, he jigged his legs up and down, in and out. 'We only have three – four days here.'

'Tell me where you are staying. I will bring you a guide.'

'We need to find a hotel.'

Now a light went on in Balram's face, in the form of a smooth glisten. This was more like it, his scene. He kept them on tenterhooks while he ran through suggestions, then dismissed them, and eventually chose. Hotel Honeymoon he could recommend confidently, he assured them, because it was where his cousin brother was manager. They would have every comfort there, and security. He had them write out the address and directions on a piece of paper. 'And tomorrow I will bring someone there, a guide.' He saw the horizons open out, thinking of all the relatives for whom he could do a favour, who would then be beholden to him, and began to smile. These city types, he could mould them like putty in his hands.

When they had carried out their bags and got into the jeep, he cleared their table, flicked it over with his dishcloth, now richly and satisfyingly blackened, and took the dishes behind the shack where a tap ran onto stones. He could close the place now with a sense of a day well spent.

The girl Shalini protested on seeing Hotel Honeymoon and did not want to dismount from the jeep, but they pointed out how late it was and how unlikely they were to find anything else at this hour. She went into her room sulkily, making Chand feel guilty, but not Bhatia. Bhatia had a strange sliding smile on his face and Chand could almost see the obscene thoughts behind it. He began removing his shoes, his clothes, reluctantly, while Bhatia stretched out on his cot under the light bulb that hung from the ceiling, flies adhering to its whole length.

On the other side of the partition wall – it was scarcely more than a screen – they could hear the girl undressing, item by item. Chand could see Bhatia imagining what those items were. He gave a snort of disgust, but could say nothing: the screen did not provide privacy of speech any more than of action. He threw himself onto his cot so that the strings creaked, and folded his arms across his chest: somehow he had to endure the night. 'Bloody Balram,' he muttered before he shut his eyes to its irritations.

In the morning Balram appeared at Hotel Honeymoon as the film crew were drinking tea and trying to eat greasy eggs with even greasier bread, hardly able to speak to one another for anger at the flea-bitten night they had endured. He brought along with him a boy. Who, what was he? An amalgam of virtues! Balram assured them: honesty, diligence, experience –

'What experience?' Bhatia interrupted, discarding the hopeless breakfast and choosing a cigarette in its place. 'At what? What has he done?'

Balram took a step back, spreading out his hands at this obviously unnecessary and offensive question. '*Everything,*' he stated with absolute conviction, and what more could be required than that?

'Such as?' The girl picked up Chand's scepticism although it was not for her to voice it. She was only the assistant, not the producer or the photographer. Still, she could not entirely suppress her opinion. It grew from the zeal she brought to the team of one whose first job it was out in the big world.

The boy stood by, his posture slack, his eyes downcast, studying his nails – some of them were flecked with crimson – as he permitted Balram to speak for him; surely it was too much to expect *him* to do so, this boy fed by his mother's hand just this morning, his hair oiled and combed by her, his clean shirt picked out for him. And now it was for Balram, his mother's brother, to do the rest and secure the job for him – if that was what they wished. What the job was had not been divulged to him, but he had heard the thrilling word – movie – in the dialogue between brother and sister last night. Movie – now he knew about movies. Once a week he bought a ticket at the Picture Palace and saw whatever it offered. The confidence that he could step into that, the world of movies, had been growing through the morning's preparations but now was somewhat reduced in the presence of these three common-looking people in their disappointing hotel. Besides, he was at a certain disadvantage here: this was the hotel where he had once washed dishes and from where he had been thrown out for unsatisfactory work. What else had they expected?

'Tell him, just tell him what you want,' Balram was saying in a loud voice as if to drown out all objections, even unspoken ones, 'and he will do.'

Having no alternative, it was with him in their jeep that they drove to the spot that Balram had picked for them as the site of the entrance to an illegal phosphate mine. The boy's name was Nakhu. He seemed in a state of disbelief that this was happening to him and whether it would be good or bad was not yet possible to tell. Could it, would it lead to his dancing on-screen with a bejewelled Bombay belle? Or would it only –

And abruptly the answer arrived: they had drawn up at the milestone Balram had suggested, under the overhang of a hill dense with shrub oak, at the edge of a precipice that dropped steeply downhill to what they could not see. It became immediately clear that the boy had not only never been here before but was incredulous that they seemed to think he had and that they expected him to dismount and let himself down a stony track that only a goat could have tackled, slipping and sliding downhill in an avalanche of rubble, taking all manner of risks with his nearly new jeans and his good shoes. He stood hesitating and teetering when Bhatia shouted, 'This is where Balram said we'd find the entrance to the mine. OK, so now take us there.'

Chand and Shalini, exchanging looks, decided to take over the lead, asking the others to follow as they stumbled and slid their way down to the promised scene of environmental degradation they might film.

The degradation did materialise, even without Nakhu's help. 'Look, look,' Shalini cried as they came upon a heap of fallen logs and charred stumps. 'Loggers have been here!'

'Then why go further?' Bhatia had already given up following them and was panting: all this exercise was not for him. 'Forget the phosphate mine, let's just film here and get it over with.'

Chand and Shalini exchanged disgusted looks. To them the effort was an essential part of their undertaking. If they had wanted to do something easy, they could have filmed in a studio, conducted interviews, put together a collage. But they had decided on filming actual sites, and sites would have to be found, perpetrators tracked down, caught red-handed if possible. Leaving Bhatia and Nakhu to follow, they continued down the slippery gravel, grasping at any bushes that seemed rooted, skirting agaves that sent out dangerously spiked spears, and got ahead – or, rather, further down the hillside.

It was dusty going and both were panting.

'Where *are* we going?' Shalini finally asked, stopping to wipe her face of perspiration. The dark glasses were proving a distinct encumbrance. 'How far did Balram say we had to go to get to the mine?'

Chand shook his head to show he didn't know but, on hearing the doubt in her voice, paused as well. It had occurred to him that the lower they went, the further they would have to climb on the way back. And even if they managed it, it was very doubtful that their equipment and equipment carriers would. 'That bloody Balram,' he swore. 'What sort of guide has he given us?'

'Where *is* he? And where is Bhatia?'

'With Nakhu.'

'Shall we wait?'

They stood and listened. Down below, concealed by the bushes, they could hear a stream running, a dog barking, someone hallooing, and up on the road they had left, a truck slowly grinding by.

'We should have asked a few more people for directions,' Shalini said.

Chand gave her a bitter look. He did not need her, his assistant, to give him advice. He was in charge of the project and it was time to take over. 'I'll go down to the river – they said there was a river – you take another direction, then double back. We'll meet at the jeep. Tell Bhatia to wait. Tell him not to risk bringing the equipment with him till we find the site.'

Shalini seemed about to protest, not sure if she wanted to be left alone, but reminded herself that Chand was her boss. He was the one who had given her this chance to show her mettle. So she nodded and struck off along a narrow track that cut into the side of the hill. Goat droppings on the stones showed it was used by others. It should be the way to somewhere.

After a while she realised what a relief it was to be on her own, not to feel the two men were keeping an eye on her, a critical, judging eye. She stopped to pick the berries of a wild raspberry bush, eating them with enjoyment even if they were tart and dry and bristly. Crushing them between her teeth, she found they revived a childhood memory of a holiday with pony rides, ice cream, a band playing in a gazebo on the Mall. Her family was not one that could often afford a holiday, it had been a rare one and memorable, but, until now, it had sunk so far back into her subconscious, she had forgotten it. Now she sniffed at the pine sap in the air with the pleasure of a renewed memory.

She almost forgot she was supposed to be looking for the entrance to the phosphate mine, or the evidence of illegal logging. She concentrated on making her way along the track, grasping at grasses here, an overhanging branch there, watching small yellow birds dart low over the lantana bushes that crowded against her legs. When her hand brushed a nettle that seemed to set it on fire, she had to stop and suck at the burn, standing under the overhang of a boulder that jutted out of the hillside, obstructing her way.

It seemed to be a natural barrier, the track was hardly likely to continue beyond it, but curiosity made her wonder if it did. The uncertainty had an edge not only of curiosity but also of fear – not exactly fear, but certainly a chill, an intimation of danger.

She would go round the rock only to see if the track continued, then turn back. As she held onto it, edging her way cautiously around, various possibilities entered her mind like brief passing shadows – of a snake in hiding, or a man with bad intentions. Or simply of getting lost. In a strange place. She was, after all, a city girl.

What she came upon was a kind of glade, so secluded it might have been undiscovered and untrodden by anyone. A wild place, half concealed from view by an enormous chestnut tree. It could have been the lair of a wild animal or perhaps even a secret hermitage.

Instead, as she peered past the overhanging branches of the tree, she saw something entirely different – a place surely ordered by human design, human hands, not nature. Nature could not have created those circles within circles of perfectly identical stones in rings of pigeon shades of grey and blue and mauve, or hoisted fallen branches into sculpted shapes, or filled the cracks in granite and slate with what seemed to be garlands of beads and petals. It looked like a bower – but of bird, beast or man? Any one of these was barely credible.

It seemed totally deserted, as composed and still as a work of art. Or nature. Or both, in uncommon harmony. The place thrummed with meaning. But what *was* the meaning? Was it a place of worship? But of what? There was no idol – unless that rock, that pattern of pebbles or that stripped branch constituted an idol. It actually seemed antithetical to any form or concept.

So what there was was a secret. Shalini gave a quiver at having found it and felt a sudden desire to give a shout, a halloo, about her find, when she became aware of someone who had been out of sight behind some rocks emerging into the glade. She caught a glimpse of a bowed head, a sleeve, a hand wielding – what? what?

She turned and ran.

When she heaved herself over the lip of the hill, hauling herself up by hands that were scratched and bleeding, and digging the toes of her boots into the gravelly earth, breathing hard from both fear and exertion, she found the jeep standing where they had left it — and desperately feared it might not be. Then, seeing Bhatia and Nakhu sitting there in sullen silence, her relief turned quickly to annoyance at the surly looks they directed at her.

'Where's Chand? We've been waiting for the two of you to come and tell us if you had found anything. We've been waiting for *hours*.'

This was unfair, if true. Heatedly, she responded, 'We thought you were to follow us!'

'With all this stuff to carry? D'you think I could let it all go and get smashed? Or stolen from the jeep?'

This made sense of course and she pulled herself up into the jeep and sat there, unscrewing the top of a Thermos to gulp water and then wipe her face with her sleeve. Nakhu watched her inquisitively now that she had removed her dark glasses. She glared at him and put her glasses back on firmly, so.

It was a long wait till Chand finally returned to report on sites of illegal logging he had found, but there was no way they could carry their equipment down there: it was unfortunate that Nakhu was only partly and not completely a donkey.

'So let's just get back to town and find the office of the timber company or the mining business, and do interviews there,' Bhatia said with all the authority of reason, and neither Shalini nor Chand could put up a protest.

Bhatia told them of a tandoori restaurant he had seen near their hotel that looked promising and later that day, having washed and changed, they went there for dinner. But when he found the food was over-spiced and greasy, it was Bhatia who complained loudest and declared he would go to bed early, which left Shalini and Chand sitting in the hissing blaze of a Petromax to finish the last of the flat, warm beer they had been served, reluctant to go back to their flea-ridden rooms at the Honeymoon Hotel.

'So, we didn't get what we came for,' Chand sighed, seeing the expedition coming to the verge of collapse.

Shalini pushed her glasses up over the bridge of her nose. 'No,' she agreed, then ventured, 'Perhaps we can look at something else now that we're here.'

'What?' Chand's snort of contempt showed what he thought of the once-alluring, now decrepit and degraded mountains.

'I saw a strange place down below, on the way downhill,' Shalini admitted in a tone of unaccustomed uncertainty. 'I could show it to you.'

'Why?'

She would have to explain. It was a strange place she had stumbled on, made entirely *of* nature, yet not *by* nature. Someone had made it. Or was making it. Some kind of artist perhaps.

Now artists were a species for whom Chand had a grudging but profound respect. What they did was what he aspired to – or once had. Then, he had imagined his training in the year at film school in Pune would lead to it. Those had been the best times he had known. But he was also bitterly aware of how far he had strayed from any artistic ideals.

'And what kind of artist would *that* be?' he growled.

'I don't know. But you've heard of that man in Chandigarh, a road engineer or something, who collected all the scrap from his road projects and built a kind of sculpture garden of it? Kept it hidden because the land he built it on didn't belong to him? Then it was found and he became famous? What's his name, do you know?'

Chand threw her a surprised and wondering look in spite of himself.

Shalini took it for an aroused interest, and curiosity. 'We could go down tomorrow and look at it. Without Bhatia and Nakhu.'

That too appealed to Chand. He had had enough of those two, and he missed his girlfriend in Delhi, the easy-going, relaxed relationship he had with her, a divorcee in print journalism with whom he could have a drink at the Press Club any evening, and who seemed content with just that, someone to accompany her. He glanced at Shalini and decided he wouldn't mind an afternoon in her company, looking for this artist, this art – whatever it was.

Bhatia had no desire to accompany them on another bone-jolting ride in the jeep to nowhere. In fact, he begged them to leave him behind – his stomach was in turmoil, he was sure it was that tandoori chicken – he couldn't think of going anywhere. Instead, he would track down 'contacts' right there in town. At the photographer's studio, his first stop since he needed some film and some lenses, he found the town was already aware of their presence and project. The photographer, chewing upon a wad of betel leaves in his cheek, asked juicily, 'You are making a movie, I hear?'

Bhatia, tired of explaining the difference between movies and television, snapped, 'What did you hear about it?'

The photographer shrugged, laughed. 'Many come to make movies here,' he said, which was no longer an original remark. 'Everybody likes the scenery here.'

'We're not interested in scenery,' Bhatia assured him and then, thinking this man might prove a 'contact', expanded: 'We are looking into illegal mines, illegal logging, reasons why this scenery of yours is getting spoilt.'

His instinct proved right. Not only did the photographer plant his elbows on the glass counter and begin giving him the inside story of the corruption and skullduggery going on in the town, but several of the men who had been slouching in the doorway, watching the street for something interesting to happen – so little did in the off-season – edged deeper into the shop and began to add their own stories, and suggestions. Bhatia grew more and more comfortable: this was his scene, this was how he had always known the project would work. Accepting betel leaves, handing out cigarettes, he asked his new acquaintances if they could set up some interviews for him.

Chand drove the jeep back to the milestone where they had first stopped. But Shalini could not find the track she had taken the day before. Of course they had to go downhill but this time the track she mistakenly chose led through a thick growth of pine and instead of coming to the glade from around the boulder, they came upon it from above, not even aware of it till they almost plunged off a shelf of rock into it, it was so well concealed in the fold between the hills by ferns and the shadows of ferns.

Shalini put out her hand to alert Chand. He stood with his hands on his hips, staring, and what he saw — what he could make out through the screen of foliage and shadows — affected him enough to make him silent, take out cigarettes and matches from his pocket, then put them away again, unlit.

'Good?' Shalini whispered, trying not to grin.

Good, bad — hardly the words that applied. He was not even sure this garden — this design, whatever it was — was man-made. How could anything man-made surpass the Himalayas themselves, the flow of hills from the plains to the snows, mounting from light into cloud into sky? Or the eagles slowly circling on currents of air in the golden valleys below, or the sound of water gushing from invisible sources above?

What he saw here, however, contained these elements, the essence of them, in constricted, concentrated form, as one glittering bee or beetle or single note of birdsong might contain an entire season.

He let out a low whistle and turned to nod to Shalini. Yes.

They drove back along the loop that ringed the hilltop to the tea stall where they had stopped on their first night for omelettes.

Nakhu had clearly kept his uncle informed of the television crew's doings. Balram greeted them with an almost familial welcome, wiping a table clear of flies for them, suggesting, 'Chai? Coffee? Omelette?'

Shalini and Chand unburdened themselves of their backpacks, and exchanged looks: shall we ask? Chand did, carefully. 'There is a garden down that hill. Whose is it? Who made it? Do you know?'

There was nothing Balram did not know: that was the reputation he liked to maintain. But here he encountered some uncertainty. His fingers searched for an answer in his moustache. 'On that hill?' he asked eventually. 'The one with the burnt house at the top?'

'We didn't see one.'

Now he could tell them about the burnt house, its reputation, its mystery. But as he was telling it, it occurred to him that he could tell them nothing about the survivor of the fire except that there was one. And what they called a 'garden' might belong to him. 'Ask Bhola,' he said at last. 'Bhola is the caretaker. He will know.'

'Where will we find him? Where is this house?'

'Nakhu is with you. Nakhu will show you the way.'

They had almost left Nakhu out of their plans, he had been of so little use. But now they had to include him. And Bhatia.

Over dinner, they listened silently to Bhatia boast about his day's achievements. 'Got some good interviews. Lots of info. You should see the men running these businesses. You won't believe, such goondas. They talked, they don't care who knows.

They've got everyone in their pockets. The whole town is making money. So we can wrap it up here, and on the way down to Dehra Dun, stop at some of these quarries – right out in the open – for background, and finish off.'

'Wait!' Shalini cried agitatedly since Chand did not.

'For what?' Bhatia turned an annoyed look at her.

She turned to Chand to explain, so he did. 'We think there might be something for us to film. Shalini showed me. It is a kind of garden. Very private, no one knows about it. But if we can find who made it – is making it – it could make a beautiful ending for the film, Bhatia. Someone who is different, someone who is not destroying the land but making something of it, something beautiful. You can see whoever it is really understands this landscape, appreciates it. We need to speak to him and see if he will let us film his garden.'

Bhatia lowered his head into the palm of his hand and ground it, groaning. Suddenly he was sick of the whole project. Everything about it was wrong, hopeless. And he needed to get home, to his wife's cooking, her care. He had had enough discomfort. Now he needed to leave.

'It's true,' Shalini broke in eagerly. 'It will make the perfect ending. First, all the bad things happening here. Then finish with something beautiful. Hopeful.'

'It's worth trying for, Bhatia,' Chand urged. It was, after all, the closest he had come in his career to art.

'And how are you going to produce this magician? Have you even *seen* him?'

'We will, we will,' they assured him, 'just give us some time,' and they sent for Nakhu. Nakhu was to lead them to the burnt house, and the magician.

Ravi was sitting on the veranda steps in the late-evening light, waiting for the homestead below to settle into its familiar pattern, smoke to rise from the thatched roof, his meal brought to him as usual, but it was Bhola who came up the path, empty-handed and strangely hesitant in manner. In addition, he cleared his throat to make Ravi aware he had something to say, and that he had been right to sense some unease in the air, something he had not been able to identify.

'There are some people here from Delhi,' Bhola began, 'they came to see me. People have been talking about them. They are here to make a fill-um.'

Ravi decided he needed to give himself time to adjust to this information. He offered a biri to Bhola although Bhola never took one from him, and lighted one himself.

'They are here to make a film,' he echoed, and wondered why he was being told this. Surely Bhola knew he had no interest at all in anything that was happening in town.

'And they wish to come and talk to you.'

It was too dark to see the expressions on each other's faces but not so dark that Bhola could not see Ravi's hand, holding the lighted biri, remain in mid-air and his entire posture freeze.

'No!' The answer finally broke from Ravi like something breaking deep inside him. 'No!'

Bhola felt compelled to offer understanding, and comfort. 'I will tell them. I will tell them you will not speak to them.'

'Yes,' Ravi said from between tightly compressed lips, a tightly constricted throat. 'Tell them. Tell them that.'

'I will tell that boy Nakhu they have engaged. I know Nakhu. Nakhu will tell them.'

Bhola meant the words to be reassuring but they did not seem to reassure Ravi. That was clear from the way he got to his feet and went blundering up the steps to his room. Bhola waited to see if he would light his lamp but he did not. The room stayed dark.

Ravi did not come out next morning. The house remained shut and silent. But at dusk, after he had brought home the goats and cow and a load of firewood for his wife, Bhola climbed the path and, on not seeing Ravi, went up the stairs and opened the door to his room. This was unprecedented: he never intruded on Ravi for any reason. But now he stood in the doorway, silently, looking in, so Ravi should be aware he was there.

'They found your garden,' Bhola told him, and he was as upset as he knew Ravi would be on hearing of the trespass. 'They filmed it, and tomorrow they want to come here. Nakhu is to bring them. They pay him.'

He could make out that Ravi was sitting at the table by the abrupt movement he made now, half rising from his chair.

'Come with me,' Bhola said and, going up to him, took him by his arm and directed him out of the room, down the steps. On the path he loosened his hold a bit but still held him by his sleeve as they followed each other down the uneven, stony track.

The dogs ran up to them in a band, clamouring. Bhola silenced them gruffly, and they turned round and led the way to the hut. Bhola's wife Manju was in the cowshed, milking the cow he had brought back from grazing. The air was thick with the smell of straw and the milk she squirted into the tin pail. The children had been whooping around, driving the chickens into their pen, but now they fell silent and stared.

Bhola took Ravi into the hut where the fire had just been lit to make the evening meal. In the semi-dark, he took down some clothes that were hanging on a line across one corner of the room and handed them to Ravi. 'Here,' he said, 'change into these. Even if you are seen, no one will think it is you. I will tell them you are my brother, visiting.' He left the room, leaving Ravi to follow his instructions, removing his khaki trousers and white shirt and pulling on Bhola's old, ragged pyjamas and a long shirt that came down to his knees. He removed his shoes and let his feet find their way into a pair of stiff, cracked leather sandals.

After a while Manju Rani came in with the milk pail and on seeing that she kept her face averted and acknowledged his presence only by drawing a fold of her headscarf a little lower over her forehead, Ravi went out into the yard among the animals. He looked for a corner where he would be out of the way. There was a log beside the cowshed and he went and sat there quietly to let the disturbance he had caused subside. The children stood and stared, not knowing what to make of all this: was he staying? Was he not going back up the hill?

When their mother called them, they went in, and Bhola came out to fetch Ravi. He indicated that Ravi was to sit beside them on the swept clay floor by the fire and passed him a tin plate that Manju Rani had filled with the potato curry she had made and some thick rotis that smelled of roasted wheat and were pleasantly charred. He ate, they all ate, no one spoke and there was no sound other than of eating and the occasional crackle of the fire. Its smoke thickened the darkness, making the darkness visible. No one was at ease.

Then Bhola led him out and showed him where he could wash at the pump, which he did, water splashing onto his sandals, making a puddle of mud around. Then he took him to an outhouse where stacks of firewood and implements were stored in the lower half and a ladder led to a shelf where there was hay and straw for the cow. Bhola had already been there and laid a rough wool blanket to make up a bed. Ravi, visibly relieved to find he was not expected to sleep with the family in the main hut, impulsively turned to thank Bhola, or in some way express his gratitude, but could not overcome his reserve, and simply nodded in acceptance of all he had been given. Bhola neither expected words nor required them and left him there.

Bhola's sons brought news to their father of the film crew's movements – down in Ravi's glade or up on the hill and around the burnt house. The children followed them around, fascinated, ready to hoot and guffaw, till they were called away roughly by Bhola who did not pass on any information to Ravi, telling him only 'It is better that you stay here. Till they are gone.' He found Ravi a Himachal cap such as he wore himself, with a band of red velvet on grey felt, to put on his head. It completed the disguise.

All day, while Bhola was gone with the beasts and the boys were supposedly at school but in truth up on the hill, Ravi had nowhere to go and nothing to do. He sat on the log by the cowshed, watching the chickens pick at grains and the insects they found among the stones, or rising up in sudden flurries of beating wings and frightened squawks at the shadow of an eagle crossing their earth, and Manju Rani going in and out about her chores, her head tied up in a long Himachal scarf and her eyes averted from him. Bhola had brought her back from Tehri as a bride; it had marked the end of his boyhood, of catapults and cricket games. After that he had been a house-holder, with responsibilities, and Manju Rani clearly had hers. Ravi never looked directly at her but was aware of her movements as she filled a bucket at the pump or clambered up the hillside to cut grasses for the goats with her curved scythe, tossing them into the basket strapped to her back. Her youngest child, a girl of about four, followed her around. Her feet were always bare, her nose was always running, her flowered frock filthy as was her hair, but her face was as round and pink as a rose in bloom. Mostly she clutched at her mother's kameez and followed her, but sometimes she broke away and came to study the man seated on the log, wondering at his stillness and silence in the midst of such continuous sound and movement. Her mother would call her sharply and she would run away, laughing.

It was a long time since Ravi had been around a woman. His mother, his female relatives in Bombay, Miss Wilkinson the last. He had no way of making any connection with those in Bhola's family but he knew he did not want to: they in no way compensated for what he had lost – his space, his enclosure, the pattern and design he had created, was creating within it. Would those barbarians from the city have stepped on it? Touched it, broken and wrecked it? Their gaze alone was a desecration. Then there were all the natural changes that were wrought daily and nightly by a passing breeze, a fall of leaves, a dwindling and dying of what had been fresh and new the day before, or else the eruption of the renewed and unexpected – and he was not there to observe and mark and celebrate them. He knew he would never go there again. It would revert to wilderness. His longing to resume what was his real life was left smouldering inside him like a match blown at but not put out. Brooding, he sat studying his hands as if they were all that were left to him now that he had nothing to work on.

Then, after a glass of tea and some bread in Bhola's hut one morning, after everyone had gone their separate ways, he saw that Manju Rani had left an empty matchbox on the clay hearth. He picked it up and went outdoors with it in his hands. It was his way, to observe and study. Seating himself on the log in his corner, he slid the flimsy container open and studied its emptiness with his habitual concentration. It might have been a crib, a cradle – but to hold what? Looking around for something small enough to fit in it, he found a sliver of bark and a scrap of moss but they left room for more. In the ground at his feet he spied a fragment of quartz that could be added. He slid the box shut and put it in the deep pocket of his shirt. All day long he reached to touch it, finding there a source of contentment and wonder at what other collections might be made.

He began to look out for empty matchboxes. Each offered a world of possibilities for the minute objects and the patterns he could make of them, patterns that he could alter endlessly as pieces of coloured glass can be shifted in a kaleidoscope. Lying open, they revealed themselves like constellations in the night. Shut in a box, they became invisible. And he could carry them on him, keep them to himself; no one would know.

Up at the burnt house, the film crew prowled around with their camera, searching for the hermit. From the veranda they could look down at the clearing, at Bhola's hut, the chickens picking around it, Manju Rani going in and out with armfuls of grass, her child in a pink frock following, a man seated by the cowshed, idly, a dog asleep in the sun.

'There's no one there,' Bhatia pronounced authoritatively. 'He's gone.'

Crouching around the projector later in the back room at the photographer's, they viewed the film they had shot 'in the garden' as Shalini called it. It was a scene drained of life, with neither colour nor fragrance nor movement. Tree, rock, leaf, stone, together or separately, they remained lifeless, the backdrop of a stage on which nothing happened.

The spool unwound with a long, rasping whirr, and its last flashes and symbols vanished into the dark. They remained crouched, unwilling to turn on the light and face each other.

Finally Bhatia said, 'We can't use this. Who would want to watch it? We'll just have to throw it away. It's dead, a dead loss, a waste of time.'

Shalini turned to face him, her face full of protest, but Chand merely sighed, accepting defeat. She realised he would not fight.

As they went to their separate rooms at the Hotel Honeymoon with Bhatia loudly bellowing, 'We can leave in the morning! First thing! It's a wrap!' Shalini said to Chand, in a low voice, 'I *could* have made it better, if we'd only found the artist who made it to show us around and talk about it, *that* would have been the ending we needed.'

'But we didn't,' Chand said with a resigned shrug. 'Perhaps he doesn't exist.'

The jeep descended the tawny hills, curve by curve, in the wake of the dust raised by a long line of buses and trucks ahead. The air grew warmer with each turn. The pine trees grew fewer, the grasses drier.

The traffic moved sluggishly, then came to an abrupt halt. Chand braked sharply to avoid crashing into the truck in front. At the bend two or three men appeared, waving red flags. Their appearance was followed by a series of dull thuds that seemed to come from inside the hill, rocking the jeep on its wheels. White dust spouted into the air, spreading in balloons and descending in parachutes, so thick it caused everyone to cough and choke.

All traffic had halted, exhaling fumes that added to the dust cloud. Bhatia jumped out of his seat – now that they were on their way back, he seemed filled with energy and determination – and joined some drivers who had climbed out along the verge. As Shalini and Chand watched, still half blinded by the explosion, they heard him give a shout and saw him throw out his arm, pointing downwards like an explorer who had made a discovery.

With reluctance and resentment, the two got down to join him and follow the direction of his pointing finger. The shelf on which they stood seemed dangerously precarious: right under it they could see great gashes that had opened out into caverns of white limestone. Even as they stood staring, another explosion went off and more white dust came boiling up towards them while echoes of the dynamite blast continued to reverberate.

Once those died away, men were seen to detach themselves from the hillside on which they had been crouching, their hair and clothes cloaked in white dust that made them look like ghostly figures in a photographic negative. With pickaxes and shovels, they began to dig, hammer and excavate.

Shalini turned away, closing her eyes to the grit and dust,

and Chand doubled over, coughing, but Bhatia was triumphant. 'That is what we need for a finish!' he shouted. 'Get the camera, let's shoot!'

A line of trucks went rumbling down a newly made track into the gully, and the ghost men below began to load them for the journey down to the plains.

ACKNOWLEDGEMENTS

Grateful thanks to Alison Samuel for her generous giving of time, attention and insight to the book through its several stages.

To Deborah Rogers for her loyal support through the years and yet another book.

Also to Jane Robison of Casa Colonial in Oaxaca, Mexico, and to Eve Halpern and Cris Sandoval of Casa Werma of Patzcuaro, Mexico, for so hospitably and protectively providing quiet spaces in which to work. *Gracias*.

The English language translation 'Everness', from *Selected Poems* by Jorge Luis Borges, edited by Alexander Coleman (New York: Viking, 1999), p.227; translated by Alastair Reid. Permission by Alastair Reid, through the Colchie Agency, New York. All rights reserved.